I Wish You Were My

Boo: A Tragic Love Story

By: Shanice B.

To Keep Up With My Latest Releases Please Sign Up To My Mailing List Below...

www.shaniceb.com

Books By Shanice B.

KISS ME WHERE IT HURTS (1-3)

HE LOVES THE SAVAGE IN ME: A TWISTED LOVE AFFAIR (1-2)

LOVE, I THOUGHT YOU HAD MY BACK (STANDALONE)

MARRIED TO A DEKALB COUNTY BULLY (STANDALONE)

ALL I EVER WANTED WAS YOU: A TWISTED LOVE STORY (1-2)

FEENIN' FOR THAT DOPE DICK (AN EROTIC SHORT STORY)

NO ONE HAS TO KNOW: A SECRET WORTH KEEPING

MEET ME IN MY BEDROOM: A COLLECTION OF EROTIC LOVE STORIES (VOLUME 1&2)

ALL I NEED IS YOU: A CHRISTMAS LOVE STORY (STANDALONE)

Synopsis

The day that Arianna said the words 'I Do' she knew she was making a mistake. She didn't love Dontae but was forced to marry him because her mother wanted her to (secure her bag) for her future. Unhappy and depressed Arianna confides in her best friend Jaleesa about her loveless marriage, hoping her best friend can help her in some way.

As Jaleesa listens to Arianna whine and complain about Dontae, she finds herself becoming infatuated with her best friend's man. He is everything that she ever wanted, and she wants him for herself.

Once Jaleesa learns that Arianna is planning to leave Dontae, she decides to make her move and seduce him, but the happily ever after that she expects to have with her best friends' man doesn't go as planned.

Will Jaleesa be able to get the man she always wanted, or will her heart be shattered to pieces?

I Wish You Were My Boo is a tragic love story that tells a story of just how far someone will go for the sake of the four-letter word L.O.V.E.

Arianna

I had only been married three months and was already praying for a damn divorce. I didn't have the love that a wife should have for her husband and probably never would. As I stared at my mother, I had the urge to slap the bitch right in her perfectly made-up face. The mother who had birthed me was a ruthless bitch, who only cared about money and having power. Me marrying Dontae had nothing to do about my feelings, it was all about her and the power she wanted. What my mother wanted she always got. Black Dynasty nightclub was something that my mother wanted to be a part of and she knew selling me out was going to get her the status and the money that she always dreamed of.

My mother was fifty years old but didn't look over the age of forty. Her pretty face and toned body always seemed to pull men that were willing to do anything to be on her arm. She had been married four times and had divorced all four of them niggas only because they couldn't provide her the life that she wanted.

April 2nd was the night that Dontae and I met. My mother was with me and we were celebrating her 50th birthday. We decided to go to the club for drinks. From the very minute I set my eyes on Dontae, I knew he wasn't the one for me, but my mother gave me that look that told me that I better not fuck her scheme up. My mother was a true Aries and was always looking for ways to make everything about her and didn't give a fuck who she hurt in the process.

I sighed with heartache as I rubbed my hand through my shoulder length hair. Every time I thought back to that night, my stomach always seemed to get in knots. The fact that my mother was a businesswoman she knew when she spotted a businessman who had potential. Donate had that potential and my mother smelled the shit from the moment that we walked into his nightclub a few months ago.

The entire night at the club Dontae couldn't seem to take his eyes off me. My mother noticed it too and used it to her own advantage. Next thing you know my mother put her plan to work. In less than two months of us meeting, I was married off to Dontae, and my mother had gained equal partnership to the hottest nightclub in Warner Robins, Georgia.

What started out as a small-town club, quickly grew overnight to the most popular club for all the surrounding cities. Black Dynasty went from having a low club rate to being worth over a million dollars.

"Don't make me slap some sense into you girl," my mother hissed as she made her a drink.

As she mixed her vodka and juice, I decided it was time to speak my damn mind. I wasn't going to be disrespectful, but if the bitch got out of line, I wasn't going to show the hoe any mercy.

"I came over here to talk to you about Dontae."

My mother slammed her glass down and eyed me up.

"Don't come here complaining to me about shit."

"Will you listen to me mother. I'm not happy. I don't love him and he can't even please me sexually," I told her with every ounce of strength that I had in my body.

My mother looked at me and laughed.

"Bitch, if you don't get out my face. Do you know how much money this man is making us? Your ass over there wearing Fashion Nova right now. If I would have never pursued Dontae for you, you would be working a nine to five job for them white folks and cleaning shit off them old folks at the nursing home. I did this for us and you don't even appreciate the shit. Do you think I loved any of the men that I married? Hell to the fucking no, I ain't even love your damn daddy. I love what he could do for me. You need to start thinking like me because if you don't, you will find yourself struggling in life. You are too fucking beautiful to have a nigga stick his dick into you and not be able to support you. You need a man who can treat you like the Queen that you are. It isn't about love, it's about so much more than that," she spoke roughly.

"I can't do this shit no more, I want out," I spat at her.

My mother walked over to me and didn't hesitate to slap the taste out of my mouth.

"It's not over until I say it's over. I don't give a fuck that you don't love that nigga. Do your fucking job and make this marriage work because if you don't, you will find yourself on the fucking streets. The cars, the clothes, the jewelry will be no more."

"I don't care about any of that. I just want to be happy."

My mother shook her head at me.

"You so fucking pathetic. Like I said earlier, do your fucking job, don't mess this shit up for us. I'm his partner at Black Dynasty everything is split into half, I became a fucking millionaire in less than a year. Life is perfect. Get with the program, Arianna."

"Fuck you mother, you ain't nothing but a selfish bitch."

My mother squinted her eyes at me as she picked up her drink and drunk half of it. She placed her glass down and stared at me.

I saw nothing but evil in her eyes.

Never had my mother ever shown me any motherly love so I had no clue why all of a sudden, I expected her to start now. When she told me that she loved me, I didn't ever feel the words in my heart as being true. My mother was a bitch so trying to reason with her wasn't going to help me, I saw that shit now.

I took a few steps back and grabbed my Louis Vuitton bag off the kitchen counter and headed out her door.

"Take your ass home and suck your husband's dick, get the fuck out my face with your crying and complaining."

"He ain't got enough dick to suck," I muttered to myself as I placed my black Gucci shades over my eyes and headed towards my 2018 candy apple red Lexus. I pulled out of my mother's driveway and swerved in and out of traffic as anger consumed my body.

I wanted out and the bitch who birthed me didn't give a fuck about my life or what I wanted. I was going to find a way out of this marriage rather she wanted me to or not. The bitch was crazy out of her mind if she thought for one second that I was going to stay in a marriage with a nigga who dick game wasn't hitting on shit. The nigga dick was average, but damn, I swear I felt nothing when he slid into me. He always caught him a good nut and would leave me wanting to be fucked into a coma.

I couldn't even remember the last time I had gotten some mind-blowing sex. I needed it, like I needed the air to breathe. I pulled out my phone from my bag as I reached the stop light and called my bestie up. Jaleesa picked up on the first ring.

The sound of her moaning and screaming out some nigga's name I had never heard of made me hang up the fucking phone. I threw the phone across the seat in frustration. At least one of us was getting dicked down.

As I pulled up at my five-bedroom mini-mansion that was in Bonaire, I said a silent prayer before I stepped my fine ass out the car. It was time to face reality and get back to living the picture perfect life of the loving wife who was happy with her husband, even though I felt the complete opposite.

Jaleesa

"Baby, all I want to do is make you feel good," Buck muttered as he slid my thong off.

I grabbed a Newport cigarette and lit that bitch, just as Buck slid a finger into my wetness.

I rubbed my hand through his dreads as he played in my pussy. I watched him and smoked on my cigarette but felt no pleasure from his tongue. This was my second time trying to fuck with Buck and this was going to be the second time that this nigga tongue game wasn't hitting on shit.

I was beyond irritated because the nigga wasn't eating my pussy like I needed it to be eaten. Buck was close to thirty-five years old, I couldn't wrap my mind around the fact that this nigga knew nothing about pleasing a bitch. I have never been the type of female to boost a nigga's ego, so I quickly shoved him off me. My pussy needed a release and he wasn't giving that shit to me.

"Damn Jaleesa what I do?" Buck asked anxiously.

"It's not what you did, it's what you ain't doing nigga. You eating this damn pussy like you a damn amateur. I ain't getting no fucking pleasure."

I could tell that I had hurt his feelings, but I didn't give a fuck. When it came to getting my nut, I was very serious about that shit. Instead of telling his ass to leave, I decided to see if his dick game was better. I put my cigarette out, pushed him down on my King-sized bed, pulled his basketball shorts down, and stroked his dick with my hand.

When he began to rub his hands through my short hair, I already knew what he wanted me to do, but the fact that his tongue wasn't hitting on shit, I quickly told him to not touch me. If this nigga thought for one second that I was going to suck his dick after that lousy ass head game that he had just done, then he was sadly mistaken. If I couldn't get my pussy ate properly then there was no way I was about to give his ass any head.

I rolled my eyes as I stared down at his average sized dick. If a nigga wanted to fuck with me, he had to know how to lick my Kat, if he didn't know how to do that then I just prayed that he had a fat ass dick to make up for that disappointment.

As I slid down on his pole, his moans in my ear told me that he was enjoying himself, but honestly, I wasn't feeling the shit. I closed my eyes tightly as I began to bounce up and down on his manhood. Just when he was near cuming this nigga had the nerve to put his hands around my throat like he was beating my pussy up.

This was far from the case, but instead of pushing his hands off me, I continued to try to reach my peek. After I had finally caught my nut, I slid off his ass with a quickness and left him staring at me like I had hurt his feelings.

"Damn Jaleesa, that shit was selfish, you ain't even let me catch my nut."

I slid my tong over my fat ass as he stared at me. I relit my cigarette before I answered him.

"Oh, I ain't know you didn't nut, my bad," I said to him with a little attitude.

Buck slid out my bed and pulled back on his basketball shorts before he walked over to me.

"You a real bitch, you know that," he spat at me angrily.

I eyed this nigga up and had to catch myself. I was two seconds from slapping his ass in his mouth for disrespecting me.

I squinted my eyes at him and didn't waste time on telling his ass how I was really feeling.

"Nigga, have you lost your fucking mind? Who do you think you damn talking to? I called your ass over here to please me and you can't even do that shit right. The first time I let the shit slide, you claim you were tired and shit, but this time is no excuse. You can't please me and calling your ass over here was a mistake, now do me a favor and get the fuck out of my house."

I could see the anger in his eyes, but I didn't give a fuck. If he wanted to fight about it, then I was down to slap a bitch ass nigga if need be.

I giggled when I noticed that his hands were balled up into fists.

"Oh, you suppose to scare me?" I asked him spitefully.

"That weak ass pussy ain't hitting on shit anyway," Buck replied crossly.

"Get the fuck out nigga!" I yelled at him.

After the front door slammed, I hurried towards the living room and locked the door.

I had been knowing Buck for three years, he was a cool ass nigga, but I had learned the hard way not to ever call his ass over here when I needed some dick. The fact that this nigga was so fine and couldn't please me is what pissed me off the most. Buck was a dreadhead, tall, slim, dark chocolate in complexion and rocked a beard that was thick and black. He could pull any bitch he wanted just by how sexy he looked. Even though he was my homeboy and I had love for him, he couldn't do anything for me sexually.

Buck was the type of nigga that I could be myself with, he accepted my flaws and all. I had a terrible attitude at times, but Buck showed me nothing but love whenever he saw me. Tonight, I was beyond irritated, so him coming over here to try to fuck me and make me feel better didn't go as planned. It only pissed me off.

I headed back into my bedroom, pulled out my dresser drawer, and grabbed my dildo. I put my cigarette out and laid my ass down on the bed. It made no fucking sense that I had to finish what he started. Even though I had nutted once with him, that shit wasn't enough to satisfy me.

I slid my thong to the side and glided my ten-inch dildo into my wet

honey pot. I didn't stop fucking myself until I was drained and tired. I

pulled my toy out my love tunnel and headed towards the bathroom where

I ran me a bubble bath. After I had soaked my pussy clean only then did I

step out and dry myself off.

I headed into my bedroom afterward and dug into my closet until I

pulled out my mickey mouse grey booty shorts along with a grey tank top.

I headed towards the kitchen a few moments later and fixed me a

margarita, I needed something to calm my nerves. As I sipped on my

drink, I grabbed my phone and didn't hesitate to shoot a text to my best

friend Arianna a few moments later.

Jaleesa: I called Buck ass over here to eat my pussy and it wasn't hitting

on shit. I sent his ass home.

I shook my head as I exited out the text message and headed back to my

bedroom. I already knew Arianna was going to joke my ass for at least a

damn week. Anytime I had a bad sex experience she joked my ass.

Arianna and I had been best friends for almost three years. I met her at

Summerhill Nursing home. We were both CNA's at the time and worked the same shift. We were the only two who were in our twenties, everyone else was in their forties, and felt they were better than us. Whenever something got fucked up on our shift (which was the night shift) it was always either one of our faults. At first, we both let the shit slide, but once it got to the point that we were about to lose our jobs, we both knew we needed to do something about the hating ass bitches that we were working with.

Arianna had my fucking back the entire time she was there, now that she had gotten married to Dontae and was living the good life, I was stuck in that hell hole and mingling with them old ass bitches who didn't like me.

As I sipped on my drink memories of the day of Arianna telling me she was getting married began to flash back ever so clearly The fact that I had never met the nigga really put me in my feelings because Arianna and I were like sisters, we didn't hide shit, so knowing she was dating someone and I didn't know them really hurt me.

Once Arianna told me what the deal was about her mother hooking her up with Dontae because of her money hungry ways, that's when all the pieces began to fall into place.

Arianna's mother was the Queen of Gold-digging and was always trying to find the next nigga who had more money. The bitch had been married close to five times and was probably looking for her sixth husband. When Arianna told me about Dontae, I knew instantly without her telling me that she didn't love this man and didn't want to be with him, but instead of Arianna standing up to her mother, she went along with her mother's scheme of securing a bag.

Arianna wasn't any longer working at the nursing home with me, instead, she was pushing a 2018 candy apple red Lexus and was living in a mini-mansion in Bonaire which was a town outside of Warner Robins. The little bitch had gotten lucky and didn't know how good she had it. She no longer had to push the clock for the white man, instead, all she had to do was stay home and look pretty. Her husband Dontae was a fucking millionaire after him and Arianna's mother partnered together to start the nightclub Black Dynasty.

If I had a mother like Arianna's, I would have taken advantage of the shit. Even though Arianna's mother could be a bitch, she was looking out for her daughter as well as herself. I didn't have a damn mother like that.

My mother had been abusive as fuck and was a drunk, when I reached the age of sixteen, I ran away from home, and never looked back.

To this day, I still can remember walking home from school and finding my mother in a drunken slumber. I tried to wake her only to be cursed out and called every name in the book that wasn't holy. I walked away from her that very day. I didn't know my daddy, so I had no one on this Earth I felt loved or cared about me. I was placed in a group home at the age of sixteen. I hated it but worked my ass off to get the fuck out of there. I finished high school and went off to college. I decided to do something in the medical field because I honestly felt like helping people was the only way to release the pain and anger that I felt inside.

Even though the pay was shitty, I got pleasure in knowing that my mother was one day going to end her ass up in the exact same nursing home that I worked at and it was going to be me who was going to have to look after her. One day she was going to get her karma, I only prayed I was able to witness it.

So, as you can see, I didn't have the fairytale childhood and I was barely making it as an adult, but through all the hard time, I never found myself jealous of any bitch, until Arianna came up in life. That's when I found myself envying her, yes, she was my bitch, and she was my bestie, but damn I wanted the life she hated so badly. I took the last sip of my liquor and placed my glass on my nightstand. I closed my eyes, so I could rest them, but eventually fell into a deep sleep.

Dontae

Being married was a wonderful feeling, but if you weren't married to the right person, it was going to feel as if you were in hell. The first time I met Arianna I fell for her. She was so fucking beautiful and caught my attention in a club filled with nothing but pretty bitches. It was something about her beauty that was raw and natural was what drew me in. She didn't have to cake makeup on her face as most women did, instead, she was naturally beautiful and that was what I fell in love with.

Arianna was the color of milk chocolate, medium in height, she was thick in all the right areas, and had medium length hair that stopped at her shoulder. The first time that we met, I stood around and watched her for a while before her mother walked over and introduced us both. I was grateful for her mother at that time, because if she wouldn't have been there, I don't even think Arianna wouldn't have even glanced my way.

With the help of her mother, I had made Arianna my wife, but keeping my marriage alive was the only issue. I was giving Arianna the world but still, I got nothing but coldness from her. I wanted to please my wife, but everything I tried to do to prove my love for her, it went unnoticed. I busted my ass every single day running Black Dynasty and bringing in so much money she could swim in it. But material things weren't what Arianna was seeking, she was seeking more than that and my heart ached for her love and approval.

All I wanted was to be loved by someone and it was heartbreaking to know that the woman I wanted to spend the rest of my life with didn't feel the same. I blamed this empty feeling and the hardship of my love life on my childhood. Growing up, I didn't know my mother, my father once told me that she had run off and had left me with him to raise. Just knowing that a woman who had given birth to me didn't love me enough to stick around fucked with me. I never got over the hurt of not having that mother's love that every child craved. Every day when I would get home from school, I would sit by the window and pray that my mother would come back to me, but she never did. I finally gave up when I reached the age of eleven and began to search for love in other places. I had been in so many relationships and they all had failed miserably. I gave so much to all of them only to feel empty and used inside. The only person who ever showed me love was my father. Even though my mother had up and left him he still worked his ass off to take care of me and give me the finer things in life. I went to college for business and finally put my education to good use just before my father passed away from heart failure.

I still felt pain inside, because not only did I lose my father, but I lost the one person who loved me through my flaws and all. My father could have walked away from me just as much as my mother, but he stood by me until he took his last breath. When he passed away, I thought I was going to die right along with him, but instead of falling into a deep depression, I took the money that he had been saving since I was a year old and invested it into my club to make it better. Before I invested into Black Dynasty, it was barely getting noticed, but after I redesigned it, Black Dynasty became popular, and that's when all my dreams became a reality. Even though I wasn't poor and had everything in this world, I still didn't have a woman by my side who was willing to give me her all. I craved a connection with my wife, only to be rejected.

As soon as the front door opened, I quickly cleared my mind. I stood up and from the chair that I was sitting in and embraced my wife in a hug. She pulled away from me and told me she was going upstairs. I pulled her back towards me and that's when I noticed the pain in her eyes. She had been crying and her mascara had smeared down her cheeks.

"Baby, what's the matter? What's bothering you?"

"I just left my mother's house, we had a slight disagreement."

"What about?" I asked her curiously.

"Do I need to go talk to her?" I asked her with concern in my voice.

She chuckled at my question.

She snatched away from me and headed up the long flight of stairs towards the master bedroom, in silence.

I rubbed my hands through my long dreads as I tried to think of something to cheer her up. I pulled out my cell phone a few moments later and decided the best thing to do was to take her out somewhere. She needed to get out of the house and going out for a romantic dinner sounded like a good idea.

After making reservations with LongHorn Steakhouse, I headed up the stairs to tell Arianna the news. I knocked a few times on the bedroom door, before she screamed to leave her alone.

"Baby, calm all that shit down. You need to shower and get dressed. We're going out to dinner in a little bit. I made reservations at LongHorn Steakhouse."

The door opened a few moments later and that's when Arianna finally appeared.

"I don't feel like going anywhere," Arianna mumbled.

"You may not feel like going anywhere, but I refuse to have you stuck in this house all day mopping and crying. Whatever you and your mother got into it about will pass over. Let's enjoy ourselves," I whispered into her ear before placing a tender kiss on her forehead.

Instead of fussing with me and rejecting my offer, she nodded her head in agreement.

"Give me an hour, I will be ready by then."

"Okay," I replied as I watched her head into the bathroom.

I walked towards my closet and pulled out a pair of khaki pants, a black polo shirt, with a pair of black Jordan's. I pulled my long dreads up in a piece of thick rubber and sprayed on my favorite Gucci cologne. I then headed to the next bathroom that was located right across from our bedroom. As I stood inside the shower and as the hot water washed across my body, thoughts of what I was going to do after dinner began to weigh heavily on my mind. A new movie called Bird Box had just come out on Netflix, so watching that after dinner seemed like something that we could do.

After I had stepped out the shower, I headed back in the bedroom. No words were really spoked as Arianna and I got dressed. I watched her as she slid on her black Fashion Nova dress and slipped on her red stilettos.

"Damn, you are looking fine as hell," I told her as I walked over to where she stood.

"Thanks," Arianna replied dryly.

Thirty minutes later, Arianna grabbed her purse and we headed out the door. (*Ella Mai*) blasted from the speakers as we headed over to Watson Blvd to eat.

After we had reached LongHorn Steakhouse, we headed inside. The waitress who looked as if she was in her late forties, took us to a booth table and took both of our orders before leaving us alone.

"Baby, we really need to talk," I said to Arianna.

She looked at me and rolled her eyes.

"Not right now Dontae, I just want to enjoy this dinner."

I nodded my head at her as I watched her play with her phone.

"I don't know why you are so cold to me, I work hard to make you happy and still you aren't satisfied."

Arianna squinted her eyes at me.

"Dontae, don't think I don't appreciate everything you do for me, it's just I'm not ready for any of this."

"What do you mean? All I ask you to do is talk to me. Tell me what you're thinking."

Arianna bit down on her lip before she finally spoke her mind.

"Dontae, I'm not going to sugar coat shit, I'm going to keep it real with you. Marrying you was a mistake."

I was just about to speak but she cut me off.

"Will you let me fucking talk, please," she told me with pain in her voice.

"Marrying you wasn't my choice, my mother pushed this shit because she saw the potential of what you was one day going to be. How in the hell do you think your club is doing so well and making so much money? My mother is smart as fuck and knows how to make money. She saw you as someone who could be worth millions and she snatched you up at that very second. Marrying you wasn't my choice, but she figured that you and I could really be this successful couple, but she didn't fucking think about my feelings on this shit, not one time did she ask me if I wanted any of this. I was happy being a fucking CNA but no, she wanted the best for me she claims. My mother wanted the power and status and she got the shit. She sacrificed my happiness to get this shit. I care about you Dontae, but I'm not in love with you. I don't love you like a wife should love her husband."

Tears fell from her cheeks and I sat there in utter disbelief. I was far from dumb, I knew exactly what type of bitch her mother was, but I didn't give a fuck, I was willing to do whatever I had to do to pull Arianna and make her be with me. Just hearing her say that she didn't love me hurt me to my soul.

"Arianna, I understand what you saying, but you haven't given me the chance to make you fall in love with me. Give it time, we only been married three months. I want to spend the rest of my life with you, I want to have kids with you and build a family."

Arianna chuckled as she wiped her tears from her cheek.

"You can't make anyone love you Dontae, either they love you or they don't. Unfortunately, you can't buy my love for you and I can't see myself bringing kids into a marriage that I don't even want to be in. We are not ready for kids, I'm not ready for kids. I just want to enjoy life."

Instead of acting a damn fool in public I remained calm. A few seconds later the waitress came out with our food.

We ate in silence for the longest time before she finally began to talk. I'm not going to lie, to learn that the woman you loved and wanted to be with didn't want you and didn't even want to have your seed was a painful feeling. I felt as if I had died inside, but I couldn't let my emotions get the best of me.

"Dontae, all I'm asking is for you to divorce me. If you still want to do business with my mother, cool, I don't give a fuck, I'm not trying to stop you from getting money, I just want to be free of this sham of a marriage."

I placed my fork down and pushed my plate to the side as I stared at her.

"Look, I'm not fucking divorcing you and don't ever ask me ever again. We married for life. I love you, Arianna, I fell for you when I first laid eyes on you. You may not feel the same right now, but one day you will. I know your mother pushed us to marry, but that was the best decision that she ever made for you. I'm a good man, I will take care of you and love you until either you or I leave this fucking Earth."

Arianna closed her eyes for a few moments before opening them.

"Don't do this to me," she murmured.

"What am I doing? I'm only giving you the love that you deserve. You won't ever find another nigga like me."

"I don't want this?" Arianna cried out.

"Well, you got it, make the best of it."

Arianna stood up and grabbed her purse.

"I can't let you go Arianna, I'm sorry," I told her truthfully.

"Don't worry, if you don't want to divorce me, I will divorce your ass."

As Arianna walked briskly out of LongHorn, I sat there and felt as if someone had smacked my ass into another world. I grabbed the check off the table, left the waitress a twenty-dollar tip, and headed to the front to pay the bill.

After the bill had been paid, I walked towards my 2018 BMW and slid inside.

Instead of Arianna and I talking about our problems, she decided to shut me out, and talk to her best friend Jaleesa the entire ride back home. When we pulled up at our crib, we hopped out, and headed inside. Arianna was still talking and laughing into the phone and acting like I didn't exist so in order to get her attention I snatched her phone out her hand and told Jaleesa that Arianna was going to call her back later.

"What the fuck is your problem?" Arianna asked me angrily.

"Our night is not over with."

"Yes, the fuck it is. We went to dinner and we talked. Now give me my phone back!" Arianna yelled.

I shook my head no and that's when Arianna snatched her phone from my hand.

She was just about to head up the stairs when I snatched her by her arm.

"Come and see this new movie called Bird Box with me."

"Jaleesa and I already seen it last week," Arianna spat nastily before she snatched her arm out of my hand.

I stood there dumbfounded as she headed upstairs. The sound of the door slamming told me that she was done talking for the night.

Arianna

I didn't love Dontae and never would. There was no way in hell I could train myself to love him, when he didn't move me sexually. I didn't give a fuck about his dick being small because small dick needed love too, but there was no chemistry there between us. Dontae could pull any bitch that he wanted. Bitches would drool over my husband anytime he went somewhere and here he was trying to force me to love him when he had options. He had bitches that was willing to fall at his feet and worship his ass, but I wasn't the one to do that shit.

I pulled off my clothes and grabbed one of his t-shirts out his dresser drawer. I pulled his shirt over my naked body and slid into bed. I just needed to try to relax and believe that everything was going to work out. Just when I was about to doze off into a deep sleep my phone began to vibrate on my nightstand. I grabbed it and that's when I noticed it was Jaleesa calling me.

"Damn bitch, you must be done got you some dick and sleep," Jaleesa joked into the phone.

"Bitch, hush. What do you want? It's late as hell," I said into the phone. Jaleesa huffed.

"I don't know what you got going on but it ain't late. It's only eleven." I sat up in bed and checked the time and sure enough it was eleven p.m.

"I'm at work, I just wanted to check on you after Dontae ended our conversation."

"I'm so sick of him, I want out and he won't let me."

"Boo, why would you want out?" Dontae is a good man.

"Jaleesa, will you listen to yourself. Yes, he a good man, but I don't love him. We have no chemistry and he can't even fucking please me. I want to be single. I want to be fucked into a coma and I will never have that desire for Dontae. We went to dinner tonight and I told him all this and this nigga told me that I just needed to give it time to love him. Since when it takes time to know if you want to be with someone? It's something you fucking already know."

"Look, Arianna I understand what you're saying, but bitches would kill to have a man like Dontae and you don't even want him."

The line grew quiet for only a second before Jaleesa told me she had to go.

"We will talk some more tomorrow. Come over to my apartment when you get the chance. This is some shit we need to talk about face to face."

"I will be there," I told Jaleesa before ending the call.

I laid there in bed deep in thought but quickly squeezed my eyes shut when I heard the bedroom door creak open. I laid there in bed frozen as Dontae prepared himself for bed.

"I love you, I know you may not love me now, but I promise one day you will," he whispered into my ear as he laid down beside me.

I continued to lay there frozen as his words began to play throughout my mind. I silently began to cry in my head because Dontae was determined to make me love him, and I was just as determined to break free of this loveless marriage. I didn't dare move from the spot on my side of the bed. I didn't want to give Dontae any reason to believe that I was up, instead I waited until Dontae was snoring lightly next to me before I slid out of bed and headed downstairs to sleep on the couch.

∞∞∞∞

The Next Morning...

The blasting of my cell phone woke me from a sound sleep. I grabbed my phone off the floor and placed it to my ear.

If I knew it was my mother calling, I would have let that bitch went to voicemail.

"What do you want mother, it's eight in the damn morning."

"You need to get your ass up, I set us up an appointment at noon to get us a pedicure and to get our nails done. Make sure you call Jaleesa to let her know that I booked her an appointment as well. I believe it's time that we have a girls day out."

I rolled my eyes as she continued to talk about the plans that she had for the day. After she realized I wasn't in the mood to talk she finally switched the subject towards my husband.

"Is Dontae home with you?"

"Yes, he's upstairs sleeping."

My mother clicked her tongue before she started to go in on my ass.

"I know damn well your ass ain't sleeping on the couch instead of lying next to your husband."

"Look, what I do with my husband is my business. You can't run shit over here mother. Its way to fucking early to hear you lecture me about what I need to be doing with that man upstairs, I will see you later this morning at the nail salon."

"Arianna, you better not hang up this fucking phone."

I wasted no time to end the call. My mother wasn't talking about shit. I already knew I was going to get an ear full later that morning at the salon. Instead of trying to fall back to sleep like I so desperately wanted to, I made sure to shoot Jaleesa a text message to let her know that we were going to have a girl's day out and she was invited.

Jaleesa sent me a few smiley faces before letting me know that she was down to come along. I gave her the time of our appointment and laid my ass back down.

A few hours later, I woke up to the smell of breakfast being cooked. I stretched and yawned as I slid off the couch and stepped into the kitchen. I stood there and watched as Dontae prepared our breakfast.

"Good Morning, sleepy head," Dontae said as he glanced up from stirring the eggs.

"Morning," I replied back.

I walked over to the kitchen island and took a seat in one of our bar stools as I waited on him to finish cooking. My stomach growled as the smell of eggs, bacon, and grits filled my nostrils.

"When I woke up this morning, you weren't sleeping beside me," Dontae said to me as he poured me a hot mug of coffee.

"I couldn't sleep so I went downstairs," I lied, just as I put the coffee mug to my lips.

Dontae didn't speak for the longest time, so I assumed he was deep in thought. To be honest, I wasn't in the mood with talking anyway. Ten minutes later as we dug into our food, I told him about the girl's day out.

Donate didn't hesitate to pull out his wallet and slid me some cash across the table. I stared at the money before I grabbed it and stuffed it into my bra. We continued to eat until both of our plates were empty and our stomachs were full. I was just about to head upstairs to get dressed when I noticed that Dontae's eyes were watering as if he was near tears.

I didn't mention any of this to him because I didn't want to find myself stuck in an emotional conversation with him, that was only going to make things worse. Instead of trying to console him, I headed upstairs to get my day started.

I pulled up at the nail shop around the same time that Jaleesa pulled up. I was grateful because I wanted to talk to her alone before my mother came along. Jaleesa slid into my car and lit her a cigarette as I poured out my heart to her.

She didn't interrupt, she only listened, as I told her about the talk that Dontae and I had over dinner.

"Jaleesa, I don't want kids with a man I don't want to be with."

Jaleesa stared into my eyes as I tried to express myself.

"Arianna, I understand what you're saying, but you ain't thinking clearly. You don't want to live like me, jumping from man to man in hopes of finding Mr. Right. You have a great husband, there ain't any good men left out here. These single men ain't hitting on shit, all the decent men are either married or in a committed relationship. You see the type of niggas I'm left to fuck with? They ain't trying to settle down and have shit with no bitch. They out here fucking bitches and making false promises that they know they can't keep. I think the best thing you should do is work on your marriage. These men don't love nobody out here, at least you have a man who willing to give you the world."

I listened to everything that Jaleesa was saying, but I knew deep in my heart that the feelings that I had for my husband wasn't going to change.

"Jaleesa, I'm holding Dontae back from him finding that one bitch who will love him. I ain't that bitch, I would be wrong to keep him tied down to me, when I know, I don't mean him any good."

Jaleesa took the last puff of her cigarette and threw it out the window before asking me what I was going to do.

I smiled at her weakly.

"I told him last night at dinner, if he doesn't divorce me, I will do it myself."

Jaleesa was just about to say something, when my mother tapped on my car window.

The conversation was far from over, but right now, I had other shit to deal with.

The conversation between us three started out light as we got our nails done. By the time we started to get our feet done, that's when all the nice shit flew out the window and my mother geared the conversation towards me and my fucked-up marriage.

"While you up there complaining and moping about your marriage, I hope you trying to secure your bag."

"What in the hell are you talking about mother?" I asked her as I popped open both of my eyes.

"When are you going to start popping out some grandbabies? Having kids by him will be securing your bag for your future."

I looked over at Jaleesa and saw the grin on her face. She was really enjoying this shit.

I rolled my eyes and closed my eyes back before I decided to tell my mother the fucking truth.

"There will be no grandbabies, at least not with him. I don't want to have kids, because that will make him always be a part of my life, and mother, I don't want him anywhere in my life."

"You're so fucking hardheaded and naïve as hell. I don't know who you act like, but it isn't me. If I wouldn't have pushed you out of my pussy I wouldn't even believe that you're mine."

"Well, mother, I hate to disappoint you, but you and I are different people. You want power, money, and control. I don't want to be associated with any of that shit. I was fine working with Jaleesa at the nursing home."

Mother scuffed.

"Baby, you too good to be wiping old folks' shit. Jaleesa no offense to you," my mother added

"None taking," Jaleesa mumbled.

My mother sighed.

"Jaleesa acts more like my daughter, then you sometimes," my mother said spitefully.

Were my feelings hurt by her comment? Not even a little bit, even though she was my mother I was nothing like her.

"Jaleesa, I haven't forgotten about you. I'm going to find you a money maker, who will give you the world," my mother said truthfully.

I laughed.

"Jaleesa don't listen to her, find your own man, and fall in love."

"Arianna, I agree with your mother, I came from nothing. I want a man who's going to give me the world and in return, I'm willing to give him all of me, including my heart. Money will make my pussy cum for him every single night."

My mother laughed and high fived Jaleesa.

I shook my head at their ignorance. They were nothing but some money hungry whores. It took everything in my soul to not get up and walk out of the nail shop without finishing my pedicure. Instead of entertaining them, I decided it was best to tune their dumb asses out.

When our toes were done and after we had paid for our services, we headed outside. My mother kissed us both on the cheek before she slid into her Jaguar.

"Arianna, I just want the best for you," my mother told me emotionally.

"No mother you're so wrong. You want the best for yourself."

My mother shook her head at me as she slammed her car door shut and pulled into the busy Warner Robins traffic.

I headed towards my car and was just about to get inside when Jaleesa grabbed me.

"I know you may be pissed at me about what I said to your mother, but honestly, I feel the same way. Imagine growing up without shit and one day finding a man who is willing to give you the fucking world. Wouldn't you take him up on his offer?"

"I'm not judging you Jaleesa. Live your life, do what makes you happy, but I want to let you know, that money isn't everything."

"No. it's not everything, but it damn sure feels good to have it."

I shook my head at her as I waved her off.

"You want to head to the bowling alley to play a game or two?" Jaleesa asked.

Even though my mother had ruined my day with her lecture about my life, I decided going out with my bestie would cheer me up. There was no point in rushing home, I didn't want to be around Dontae or hear him beg for me to love him. Going bowling sounded like the best option for me.

"I will meet you there," I told Jaleesa as I closed my car door shut.

Ten minutes later Jaleesa and I were pulling up at the bowling alley and headed inside. We paid for three games, grabbed our bowling shoes, ordered us a snack, and went to find us a lane to sit at. I won the first game and Jaleesa won the second game. We were on our last game when someone tapped me on the shoulder.

I turned around and came face to face with a man who was so sexy that I found myself not able to tear my eyes away. He was the complexion of a caramel milky way, he rocked a low cut with his sides faded, his teeth were pearl white and straight. He was dressed in a pair of jeans, a black t-shirt, with a pair of black Air Forces.

"Hey beautiful, how are doing today?"

"I'm doing okay," I heard myself say.

"My name is Ken. What's your name beautiful?"

"I'm Arianna and this is my best friend Jaleesa," I told him as I pointed towards my bestie.

His eyes were a brown hazel and I felt as if I could get lost in them.

He spoke to Jaleesa, but his eyes never left my own.

"I'm a few lanes down and couldn't help but notice you over here. I wanted to get see if you were interested in us getting to know each other better."

I was just about to speak but Jaleesa beat me to it.

"Um, she's off limits, she's a married woman," Jaleesa said just as she grabbed my left hand to show my wedding band.

I snatched my hand from her grasp, but it was too late, the damage had been done.

"I'm sorry for disturbing you, I'm not interested in messing with another niggas property. He's a lucky dude, I hope he treating you like the Queen that you are."

My whole body felt as if it was on fire as he caressed my face with his hand.

"Nice to meet you, Arianna."

I watched him as he headed back over to his lane and instantly my heart felt as if it was going to break in half.

"Why the fuck did you do that?" I asked Jaleesa with attitude.

"I did it to protect you and what you have with your husband. You ain't going to find another Dontae."

"Bitch, if Dontae so damn good then, by all means, take that nigga off my hands. You can have his ass, maybe then he will let me move the fuck on," I replied angrily.

"You can be such a bitch at times," Jaleesa said crossly.

"Bitch, I could have gotten his number and be getting some new dick later tonight, and you just fucked it all up for me. Since when do bitches or niggas care about anyone being married?"

"Apparently, that nigga cares because he gone in the wind now. Bitch, you got dick at the crib, take your ass home, and pop that coochie."

"I would go home, but what's the point, his dick ain't hitting on shit."

Jaleesa

A Few Days Later...

Everyone always wanted what they couldn't have but I was the type of bitch that was going to get everything that I had dreamed of and more. As I applied lipstick to my full lips, I stared at myself in the mirror. I was going to make Dontae mine and there wasn't shit anyone could do about it. Arianna wasn't thinking clearly, but I had tried one too many times to try to talk some sense into her naïve ass. The fact that she acted like she didn't care, gave me even more reason to snatch her nigga up. I didn't want to ruin my friendship with my bestie, but if I had to sacrifice my loyalty to her so I could be happy then I was willing to do just that.

To be honest, I had no clue if she was being serious about me taking Dontae off her hands and I didn't give a fuck. I just wanted a nigga who was going to spoil me and take care of me, she had all of this and still wasn't satisfied. Some bitches just were too dumb to know when they had a good thing. What was the point of letting Dontae suffer and allowing him to keep being rejected by Arianna, when he had a bitch like me that was willing to give him whatever his heart desired?

My green hazel eyes sparkled as I smiled deviously to myself. The plan of making Dontae fall in love with me was going to work, I just felt it in my soul. I was irresistible. I was a siren to the men who were lonely and felt unloved. I was their savior and was willing to nurture them back to health.

After I was satisfied with my appearance, I grabbed my purse and headed out the door. I slid into my 2017 Acura and headed straight towards Black Dynasty.

I pulled up at the club about ten minutes later, found me a parking spot, and waited in line for the bouncer to pat me down. Even though my feet were cramping I waited patiently without complaining. After I had been patted down and my purse had been searched, I headed inside.

Cardi B. blasted from the speakers and bitches was twerking and dancing on their niggas. Instead of heading towards Dontae's office, I decided to get me a drink just so I could calm my nerves. I ordered me a Strawberry Margarita and sipped on my drink until the anxiety that I was feeling was washed away. I lit me a cigarette and smoked half of it before dumping the remains in an ashtray that was in front of me. I slid out of the barstool on shaky feet but gained my balance as I pushed through the crowd towards Dontae's office.

A few niggas along the way stopped to try to flirt and get my number but I didn't give their asses any play. I already had the nigga that I wanted to be within my sight and there was no way I was about to let anyone distract me from making Dontae mine. As I made my way towards the back of the club, the music began to fade, and then everything grew still.

My heart began to beat erratically as I knocked a few times on Dontae's door.

"Come in!" Dontae shouted out.

I took a deep breath and exhaled before I came face to face with Arianna's husband.

"Jaleesa, what are you doing here?" Dontae asked as he walked over and embraced me in a hug.

I closed my eyes as his cologne invaded my nose.

"Is Arianna here with you?"

I pulled away from him and told him that I came by myself.

Dontae headed back towards his chair and took a seat behind his desk. As he stared at me, I felt as if he was staring into my very soul. I bit down on my lower lip as the air in the room began to suffocate me. My pussy began to sweat and my nipples began to harden from the sexual energy that I was feeling inside my body.

I took a seat in the chair that was facing Dontae and crossed my legs as I began to tell him why I had come to see him. One thing that I had learned at an early age was how to get what I wanted from a nigga. Most men where the same and could be easily tempted if the bitch knew what she was doing.

I stared innocently at him as I toyed with my fingers.

"I came here because I needed to talk to you about Arianna."

Dontae cleared his throat and appeared to be uncomfortable. He couldn't sit still, and I knew exactly why. The sexual vibes that I was giving off were affecting him just like I had hoped.

"What about Arianna?" he asked quizzically.

"She isn't happy with you Dontae. I'm sorry to be the one to tell you this but, she just doesn't see you as the type of nigga she wants to spend the rest of her life with."

Dontae sighed with frustration and I continued to talk.

"I'm her best friend and she tells me everything. She doesn't want to be tied down in a loveless marriage, she doesn't want kids, and she wants you to divorce her."

"That's not fucking happening. She won't even give me a fucking chance to prove her wrong," Dontae replied emotionally.

As I stared into his eyes all I saw was devotion and love there. Arianna was one lucky bitch and didn't even give a fuck. I would kill to have a nigga to feel this way about me, I thought to myself.

"I tried talking to her and have tried to persuade her to stay married to you, but she just isn't interested in any of this," I replied honestly.

I saw the hurt in his eyes and that's when I felt it was time to work my sex magic on him.

I slid out of my chair, walked over to him, and began to massage his massive shoulders as he confessed to me how much he wanted his marriage to work. I listened and didn't dare interrupt him until he had gotten everything off his chest.

I turned Dontae around to face me and stared deep into his eyes.

"You have so much to offer and so much love to give, don't continue to drain yourself of your affection and resources, if she doesn't want it. Save all this energy for the bitch who's going to appreciate you and be there for you."

Dontae seemed to hang on my every word, but I still could feel some resistance of him letting go.

"I just don't want to let her go," he whispered.

I shook my head at him.

"Let her go Dontae, don't trap yourself in a marriage to someone who doesn't love you. If she doesn't love you, she will not give a damn about your feelings.

I look at everything Arianna has and find myself wishing that I could get just a taste of it," I admitted to him.

Dontae nodded his head as he caressed his finger across my jawbone.

"You're so beautiful, you can have any man that you want."

I smiled at him weakly as a single tear fell down my cheek.

"The man that I want, I can't have. He is still in love with a bitch who doesn't give a fuck about him."

Dontae snatched his hand away from me and I took a few steps back.

"You don't really want me, you just trying to get in my head and seduce me so Arianna can have a good enough reason to leave me."

I stared at him in disbelief and couldn't help but laugh at his dumb ass.

Even though I knew he had every right to question my motive, I still couldn't believe that he thought Arianna had sent me to seduce him.

"Let's clear some shit up. Arianna didn't send me, I sent myself. She complains that your dick small and that you can't please her, she don't love you Dontae and never will," I told him bluntly.

Dontae was about to speak but I cut his ass off.

"I don't care if your dick is big or small. We can always do something to fix that issue. I don't want you for your dick size, I want you because I know you will forever be loyal to me and I want the stability that you can provide to me. Arianna will never love you like I can. She will never be interested in pleasing you like I will."

I walked over to him seductively and his eyes never left my body.

"I know you want me, I can feel it," I purred.

I wasted no time going in for the kill, he was weak, and I was ready to seal the deal. I caressed his dick print with my soft hands as I placed a wet kiss on his neck.

I smiled to myself when he grabbed me and placed me on top of his desk.

His lips covered mine as we shared a deep kiss. My body was on fire and I could tell that he wanted me as much as I wanted him. I pushed him off of me and shoved him into his office chair as I slid my tight spandex dress up over my stomach. I got down on both of my knees, pulled his manhood out of his navy-blue pants, and began to gently stroke his rock-hard dick.

He wasn't small like Arianna had stressed, he was average, but since she was the type of bitch who had to have at least ten inches I understood why she said he couldn't please her. I licked my lips as I slid his manhood into my wet mouth. I slurped and licked the top of his mushroom head as he moaned out my name.

"Fuck," he whispered as I slid him down my throat without gagging.

He rubbed his hands through my short hair as he worked my head in a steady motion of his satisfaction.

"Suck this dick," he kept crying out to me as I sucked the soul from his body.

Just when he was about to cum, I pulled my mouth from off his manhood and straddled him. His grunts filled my ears as I started to pop my pussy on him. He gripped my ass and bit down on my neck as I rocked his world.

I cried out with arousal when he stood up from his chair, threw all the papers off his desk, and placed me on top of it. He slid between my thighs and placed a few gentle kisses on my pussy lips before he dived inside. As his tongue sucked on my clit, I squeezed my eyes shut in pure ecstasy.

"Shit," I cried out as his tongue dipped into my honey pot.

"Fuck me," I heard myself whimper.

Dontae wasted no time as he slid his dick back into my love tunnel. He started out fucking me slow and deep, but I wasn't in the mood for lovemaking. I wanted to be fucked hard and rough.

"Fuck me harder, beat this pussy up," I instructed him.

Dontae flipped me over, pushed my legs apart, and slid into me from the back. Tears ran down my cheeks as he fucked me roughly. He made sure that I was taking all his dick by giving me deep strokes that had me screaming.

"Take this dick," he kept whispering into my ear as he fucked me. Sweat dripped down my face and my pussy was leaking my sweet nectar as he gave me all of him.

"I'm about to cum," he choked out.

I squeezed my eyes shut as my honey pot began to cream all over his dick. He slammed into me one final time before he spilled his seed into my juicy love tunnel. We detached from one another a few seconds later. I fixed my dress back over my ass and watched him as he slid his semi-hard dick back into his pants.

"I honestly enjoyed what happened," he admitted.

I held my breath as I waited for him to say more. I closed my eyes as he caressed my cheek with his finger.

"You have opened my eyes to what I have been missing. Never have Arianna ever made me feel this way."

I bit down on my bottom lip as pulled away from him.

"Now you see the difference."

"What do you mean?" he asked.

I smirked.

"Now you understand what it feels like to be fucked by someone who really wants you."

I grabbed my purse and was just about to leave his office when he grabbed me by my arm.

"No don't go, stay a little while longer."

He didn't want me to leave, which gave me the indication that Dontae had fucked and had already caught feelings.

I turned back around and walked into Dontae arms.

"I don't want this to ever end."

"It doesn't have to," I whispered into his ear.

"What are you talking about?" Dontae asked curiously.

"I'm willing to give you all of me, only if you do something for me."

"What do you want me to do?" Dontae asked desperately.

"Divorce Arianna. Make me your wife. I deserve that title, not her."

I didn't wait for his answer because I knew he was going to need time to process what had just happened between us. I felt the best thing I could do was let him think about what I was offering him. I placed a kiss on his cheek and walked out of his office. I only prayed that he made a choice very soon.

Dontae

The Next Day...

I couldn't stop thinking about Jaleesa. No matter how hard I tried I couldn't shake her from my mind. It was like I was in a dream and didn't want to ever wake from it. I knew deep down that what Jaleesa was offering me was something that I always wanted. I always wanted to be able to love and protect the woman who had my heart. The fact that Jaleesa was willing to give me her all, really put my heart at ease. All the stress that I was feeling to make my marriage work with a bitch who didn't want me was soon going to be over with, if I chose Jaleesa. So many feeling and thoughts were running through my mind, but the sound of my mother in law's voice was what snapped me out of the fairy tale dream that I was having about my future.

"Dontae are you listening to anything that I have said?" Ariella asked irritably.

"No, I just have a lot on my mind right now. Can we talk about this next week?"

Ariella pressed her lips together and placed her paperwork back in her vanilla folder.

She sighed with frustration and I ignored her ass.

I swear she could be a bitch at times. Now I understood where Arianna got her attitude from.

Ariella walked over to me and took a seat on my desk as she stared at me. Her dark eyes penetrated my soul and for a moment I had the urge to tell her to leave.

"Dontae, I know that my daughter has been giving you a hard time about this marriage and her feelings towards you, but just hang on a little more her tune will soon change. Don't let her make you feel less of a man, she doesn't know how good you are for her."

I shook my head at her statement.

"Ariella, your daughter is stressing me the fuck out. She wants out and I'm beginning to think that she is so right."

Ariella gasped and stared at me like I has slapped her.

"I thought you loved her and couldn't be without her?"

"Things have changed, why should I keep forcing my love on someone who clearly doesn't want it. I love her enough to set her free, I don't want to trap her into this marriage if she isn't happy. Life is to short, to be unhappy."

"But what about the business our partnership at Black Dynasty?" Ariella asked.

I already knew at the end of the day that Ariella only cared about her coins. She didn't give a fuck about Arianna and what she wanted. I was beginning to think that maybe cutting her out of the partnership was for the best. I didn't want to have to deal with her when Arianna and I divorced each other. I wanted all ties to be cut from Arianna and her controlling, power-hungry mother. Both were going to be dead to me when I signed my name on the divorce papers.

"Ariella, let's be real with one another, there is no point in you being my partner any longer. Arianna wants to divorce me and so should you. I think it's for the best."

"No, you can't do this to me. You can't cut me out of this club. I've worked my ass off to make this club the best and this how you going to do me?" Ariella asked angrily.

I saw the tears that were in her eyes which made my chest tighten. Never had I ever witnessed Ariella cry, so I was in shock.

"Ariella, I'm not trying to hurt you, I'm just preparing you for what is about to come. The divorce is coming very soon, I can't do this shit any longer, I hope you understand."

"You and my daughter are so fucking stupid," Ariella spat at me.

If this bitch wouldn't have been Arianna's mother, I would have smacked her ass. I was a lot of shit, but I wasn't stupid.

"Ariella, you aren't going to get far in life with that attitude you have, you rather sacrifice your daughter for money and power, you're pathetic. If money is what you want, I will write you a fat ass check, it will be enough for you to buy your ass a building and start your own business."

"You so full of shit, you going to regret this shit!" Ariella yelled at me just before she stormed out of my office.

I sat there in my office and rubbed my hands over my face as I tried to shake the stress that I was beginning to feel. I pulled out my phone a few seconds later and dialed Arianna's number. She picked up on the first ring and answered the phone dry as hell. This wasn't anything new. Just hearing the unhappiness in her voice was all I needed to give her what she wanted.

"If you want the divorce, I'm willing to sign," I spoke into the phone before hanging up.

∞∞∞

A Few Hours Later...

"What made you change your mind?" Arianna asked.

"You were right all along. Keeping you in this marriage isn't right. I love you so much, I want you happy even if it isn't with me."

Arianna nodded her head as she stared down at her baked potato and steak.

"Who is she?" Arianna asked quietly.

"Who are you talking about?" I asked her in confusion.

Arianna smirked.

"Don't sit here and play dumb Dontae, I have been around you long enough to know that you are hiding something. You even look different. You look happier. You have been fighting me hard on why we should get a divorce and now all of a sudden you're okay with it. You must have met someone you want to get to know better."

"I don't know what you're talking about," I lied.

Arianna laughed.

"I don't care who she is. I'm just glad you have found you someone else to obsess over for a while," Arianna joked.

"Your mother is pissed with me. She wants us to remain married and try to work things out."

Arianna rolled her eyes.

"That bitch is only worried about the money and the partnership with Black Dynasty," Arianna responded angrily.

"Yeah, I know. I just don't want that negative energy from around me. Once the divorce is official, I don't want nothing tying us together, so I told her once the divorce was settled that we were no longer going to be partners."

"Shit, I bet she almost had a fucking heart attack."

"She super pissed with us both."

"Well, you already know I don't give a fuck about the bitch being pissed."

"Look I'm not that cold to just divorce you and not give her anything. I told her I was going to write her a check and it's going to be enough for her to get her own building and start her own shit whatever she wants to do with it."

Arianna laughed.

"I swear you was way too nice to that bitch, I bet she still ain't satisfied."

"Nah, she left out my office mad as hell."

"That's Ariella for ya ass," Arianna muttered.

I watched as Arianna cut her sirloin steak into tiny pieces before covering it with A1 sauce. I took a bite of my baby back ribs and chewed as Arianna and I continued to discuss her mother and our divorce. After we had finished our dinner, we headed out of Applebee's, and walked towards our car.

Ten minutes later we pulled up at our house and headed inside. Arianna headed to the kitchen to fix her a drink before going upstairs to the bedroom, while I stayed downstairs to drink a beer and watch T.V. My phone vibrated in my pocket letting me know that I had a text message. My heart skipped a beat when I noticed that it was Jaleesa messaging me.

Jaleesa: Have you thought about what we talked about?

Dontae: Yes...

Jaleesa: Have you decided?

Dontae: I'm divorcing her. The process will be started asap.

Jaleesa: Good. Just let me know when something changes.

Dontae: I will keep you in the loop.

I was just about to ask her if I could come over later that night but that's when Arianna walked over to where I was sitting and took a seat beside me. I put my phone away as I sipped on my beer.

"You ain't got to stop texting whoever you were talking to. I just wanted to come downstairs, so I could watch a little T.V," Arianna told me as she flopped down next to me with her drink in her hand.

I already knew Arianna was lying. She didn't have to come all the way downstairs to watch T.V when she had one in her room. She came down here to be nosy instead.

After American Horror Story had gone off, I got up to throw my empty beer bottle in the trash, but that's when Arianna pushed me back down on the living room couch.

"Who is the bitch, that you want to leave me for?" Arianna asked crossly.

I stared at Arianna in confusion because how she was slurring her words, I knew then that whatever I said wasn't going to please her since she was drunk.

I tried to take her cup from her, but she pushed me away.

"You have had too much to drink," I told her calmly.

Arianna shook her head at me and placed her cup on the coffee table.

"Yes, I admit I've drunk over the limit, so you already know what I want."

"What do you want?" I asked her curiously.

"I want some dick, I want to be fucked hard and rough," Arianna replied aggressively.

She tried grabbing for my dick, but I pushed her away.

"We don't need to be fucking, we're divorcing each other remember."

"And, since when divorcing one another got anything to do with us both catching a nut. I just want the dick nigga, I have needs. So sit back and let me pop this pussy on you."

I stared at her in disbelief because this was going to be the first time Arianna was willing to fuck me on her own terms.

"All you need to do is get hard and let me take care of the rest."

I closed my eyes and tried to fight the urge of my erection and desire to feel her body intertwined with my own, but it was super hard.

Arianna wasted no time with unzipping my black jeans and pulling them down. I pulled off my red Chicago Bull shirt just as she pulled down my boxers. She grabbed my manhood with her hand and started giving me some sloppy head. Since Arianna and I had been knowing each other never had this bitch ever given me head this damn good.

I felt as if I was in a dream that I didn't want to wake up from. As she sucked and slurped on my dick, she gently caressed my balls as she deep throated me.

"Fuck," I heard myself moan out when she pulled my dick out her mouth and started to suck on my balls.

Just when I felt like I wanted to bust, Arianna moved away from me and undressed herself. She pulled down her blue jean booty shorts and took off her hot pink t-shirt. She pulled off her black thong and unsnapped her bra just before she slid on top of me.

Her moans were like music to my ears as she rode my dick. I held her tightly as she sucked on my neck as she popped her coochie on me.

I stood up from off the couch, pushed her back into the wall, as she wrapped her legs around my waist. I slammed into her with every force in my body as I fucked her in the air. All the hateful and mean shit that the bitch had said to me was beginning to play back in my mind. She claimed

I had a small dick and I couldn't please her, the shit was painful, but it gave me the strength to fuck her until she cried.

She yelled out my name and tried to pull away, but I held her ass firmly in position and continued to drill her up in the air. A few seconds later, I pushed her back up against the wall and slammed my dick deep into her honey pot as I could go.

She screamed out into my ear, but I didn't dare stop. I sucked and bit down on her neck just before I put her down on shaky legs. I flipped her around, as placed both hands on the wall. I slammed into her from the back as her pussy juice covered my tool. I grabbed her by her hair and drilled her until she was crying and shaking.

"I'm about to cum," she choked out.

I slammed into a few more times before I spilled my seed deep inside her hungry wet pussy.

I was so damn weak after our fuck fest that neither one of us could move. We didn't detach ourselves from each other bodies until both of us had calmed down. I slid out of her and smacked her on her ass.

I had just finished putting on my clothes, when Arianna walked over to me, and started to put back on her clothes as well.

"Never have you ever fucked me so aggressively and rough," Arianna told me as she shoved her shirt over her head.

"I'm just curious to know what has come over you. It's fucked up how you waited until we about to divorce each other, before you start showing me what that dick can do. Now you got me wondering if leaving you with whoever the bitch you trying to be with is such a good idea."

My heart began to race because I wasn't expecting to hear any of this shit. Was she truly thinking about changing her mind? I stared at her for a moment before I shook my head at her comment.

"You're not happy with me Arianna, so it's no point in staying with me now. Divorcing is what is needed."

"Divorce me if you want to, but I have the right to still get dicked down until then. I want you to continue to fuck me like you hate me. I want it rough baby, I don't want you making love to me, I want you to fuck me. It's a difference."

I stood there speechless as I watched her grab her cup off the coffee table and head upstairs. I took a seat back on the living room couch after I had finished putting back on my clothes. My mind wouldn't stop racing, Jaleesa had given me exactly what I needed to keep Arianna coming back for more. If I could change her mind and have her wanting to fuck me then I could probably change her mind about loving me. I closed my eyes and as I tried to settle my thoughts. Even though Arianna had a gleam in her eye, did I really want her to love me now that I had made plans to be with Jaleesa? My goal had once been to make Arianna fall in love with me, but the question was did I still want that?

My emotions were all over the place, but it was time that I thought about what I wanted because I couldn't just think only of myself. I had to think about Jaleesa and the proposition that she had given me. who did I want Arianna or Jaleesa only time was going to tell. I just prayed it was on my side.

Arianna

I had just pulled up at Subway when Jaleesa pulled up beside me. She stepped out her car and walked over to knock on my window. I slid out my Lexus and was just about to head inside to order me something to eat when Jaleesa stopped me.

"We need to talk first, and I don't want no one in Subway to overhear us."

I raised an eyebrow at her ass because I could tell whatever she had to tell me was serious because her whole vibe was off. I stood up against my car and waited for her to get whatever she had to off her chest.

Jaleesa inhaled and then exhaled before she finally began to tell me some shit that didn't sit right with me.

"I'm in love with someone."

I almost fell over because this wasn't something that I ever thought I was going to hear. To be honest, I never felt Jaleesa could love someone else besides me and herself. All she did was fuck niggas and dispose of them as if they were a piece of trash and it was all because none of them wanted to love on her and give her the world. Jaleesa was a smart-ass little bitch and knew that fucking over a nigga before he fucked over her was the best way to keep her heart safe.

"Arianna you're my best friend but I had to choose between our friendship or my heart desires."

I stood there confused because the bitch was talking in riddles. Jaleesa has always been cutthroat, but she was dancing around with telling me who she was in love with. I guessed she sensed that I was beginning to get impatient and that's when she finally spilled the tea.

"I fucked Dontae and I want to be with him. He knows you don't love him and never will and I promised to give him all of that and more."

I felt as if I had been smacked. When the bitch told me she had something to tell me, I wasn't expecting to hear some shit like this. Instead of being happy for the bitch, I stood there in disbelief as anger began to consume my body.

"Bitch, you slept with my fucking hubby?" I asked her angrily.

"Hold the fuck up. Why you upset. You said out your own mouth don't you don't love him, you don't want him, you want out your marriage, you didn't want his babies, and you personally told my ass at the bowling alley that I could fuck him and take him off your hands. You gave me permission to take him from you. Be honest with yourself Arianna, you don't want his ass. So, divorce him and I will take it from there."

I was so hurt and pissed that I lost all bit of control of my anger and smacked the shit out of her.

Jaleesa stood there in shock as she held her hand to her cheek.

"Bitch, what the fuck is your problem? Friends don't do shit like this. I don't give a fuck what I said to you. You're my fucking friend anyone of my exes are off fucking limits. As many niggas you have smashed and sucked how many of them did I fuck behind you? None of them. I respect you and don't want your fucking trash. Friends don't betray friends."

"Look, Dontae is a good fucking man. The men I fucked with in the past is nowhere near on Dontae's level. You never fucked any of my niggas because they ain't about shit. Dontae is a lot of things, but he is more than a piece of trash. If you don't want him, then let me have him, why torture the poor man? He told me that he will give you the divorce and it's just going to be me and him. I'm going to show you just how to treat a man like him!" Jaleesa yelled at me.

The last little bit of sanity that I had I lost it right then and there. I grabbed her by her slim neck with my hands and squeezed as hard as I could. The anger that I was feeling had to be released and I wanted to give it all to her ass. The fact this bitch had the nerve to sleep with my hubby was hurtful. I knew I had said a lot of awful shit about Dontae but at the end of the day, he still belonged to my ass. She had known me long enough to know that I didn't share anything or anyone.

Jaleesa clawed at her neck, but it only made me squeeze harder. Just when I thought I had killed her, that's when I felt someone pull me away from her. Jaleesa coughed and fell to the ground as she gasped for air.

I turned around and there stood a few onlookers.

"Is everything okay? Do I need to call the police? the man asked Jaleesa as he ran to her aid.

Jaleesa grabbed on to him as she stared at me with water in her eyes.

"No, me and my best friend had a disagreement."

I shook my head at her and laughed.

"Correction, you're my ex best friend. Do me a favor, stay away from me, and leave my fucking husband alone, because if I find out you still trying to persuade him to be with you, there will be round two bitch, next time you won't be so lucky," I spat at her before I slid back into my car and sped out of Subway parking lot.

I only had one destination in mind, I pulled out my phone and tried to call Dontae, but my call went unanswered, I threw my phone on the passenger seat and swerved in and out of traffic. It was ten thirty at night and Black Dynasty was just beginning to get crowded. I pulled up at the club and found an empty parking spot. I left my purse and phone in the car and locked the door behind me. I headed to were Dontae had his security team checking bags and purses and was just about to walk past them when one of them grabbed me.

"Ma'am, you need to go to the back of the line and wait your turn. No one enters before being checked."

"Get your fucking hands off me, I'm Dontae's wife. I'm the reason you got this fucking job."

The bouncer looked at one another in horror.

"I'm so sorry Mrs. Jordan, I didn't recognize you."

I didn't bother by even responding I had other shit on my mind. I headed inside the club grabbed me a margarita and sipped on it. I had to try to calm myself down. There was no way that I was going to go to find Dontae with the rage that I was feeling inside because it was the type of rage that would only lead to me murdering his ass. After I had finished my drink, only then did, I head towards Dontae's office.

I didn't bother by knocking, I walked up in that bitch ready to fuck some shit up.

"Arianna, what are you doing here?" Dontae asked quizzically.

I slammed the door behind me and strutted towards his desk.

"I found out some interesting news today."

Dontae stopped what he was doing and gave me his full attention.

I laughed evilly as I pulled my hair from out of my face.

"Are you okay?"

"I'm not fucking okay, not after hearing about you fucking Jaleesa. We met up at Subway to get something to eat and she spilled the tea."

Dontae didn't speak and he didn't deny the shit either, I knew from looking him in the eye that he had some serious feelings for Jaleesa, knowing this hurt me to my very soul.

"You actually leaving me for Jaleesa? All these hoes out here and you leaving me for my a bitch who was my best friend. You didn't think about how this was going to make me feel? I almost killed her ass all because of you."

Dontae stood up.

"What did you do?" Dontae asked angrily.

"Shut the fuck up nigga, your little bitch is safe," I only choked her ass out.

"Arianna why are you doing this shit, you don't want me and you don't love me. You have told me on many occasions, so why you upset about Jaleesa and I? She has shown me nothing but love, unlike you. Marrying her will be the best thing that can happen to me."

"You one dumb ass nigga, if you think for a second that hoe is marrying you because she wants you. She only wants you for what you can do for her."

Dontae walked over to where I was standing and stared at me. I saw nothing but coldness in his eyes. I felt nothing but hate radiating off his body.

"In every relationship, someone is going to be used. I don't give a fuck about her being with me for what I can do for her. I'm a good ass nigga, I promised her ass that I was going to take care of home and give her anything that her heart desired and in return, she offered me her loyalty and her heart. Unlike you, Jaleesa knows how to play the game. She not trying to just take from me Arianna, instead she giving something back in return. I'm sick and tired of trying to love you and take care of you and you treating me like I'm a piece of shit. So yes, I fucked your friend, the plan is to divorce your ass, marry her, and live life to the fullest. Baby, you must have forgotten that you ain't the only bitch in this world? So many who will love to have what you have, Jaleesa deserves me and so much more Arianna."

I felt as if my heart had been ripped out my fucking chest. He didn't sugar coat shit, he gave it to me raw and uncut and I hated him for it.

Tears ran down my face and rage filled my body. I pushed past him and destroyed his office. He only stood back and let me get all the anger out.

"Are you fucking done?" Dontae asked.

I could tell that my temper haven't even moved him, instead he stood there as if he was unimpressed.

"Finally, I see some emotions from you. It took me to leave you for your best friend to get you to show some feelings towards me."

"I hate you!" I yelled at him.

"Since you hate me so much, then you will sign the divorce papers next week."

I stood there frozen.

"I'm not signing shit," I spat at him.

Dontae smirked.

"You're really in your fucking feelings about me wanting to be with Jaleesa. I would feel sorry for you, but I don't. You don't have to sign the papers luv, the divorce will carry on without your signature. That's what my lawyer for."

I was super pissed and cursed myself for not bringing some type of weapon with me. The way I was feeling I wanted to fuck his ass up. But as I stared at him, I realized that he wasn't even worth going to prison for.

"You don't love me, but you don't want me to leave you for someone who will love me? Honestly, I don't get your logic of thinking," Dontae told me irritably.

"It's a girl code. NO bitch is to fuck with their best friends ex. It's off limits. She broke the fucking code when she fucked you."

"NO Arianna, you broke the fucking code when you complained and cried to her by how unhappy you were with me and how you wanted out of this marriage. You are grown as hell, you know how bitches work, Jaleesa seen that you wanted out and has helped you find a way. She is taking me off your hands. NO longer will you suffer and be tied down to a nigga you don't fucking love or want to be with. Take the L and let's move on with our lives."

I tried to speak but I couldn't. I was tongue-tied because I knew he was correct. What I was hurt over the most was that Jaleesa had betrayed me.

"A nigga is always going to be a nigga. They always going to find some reason to fuck off, but Jaleesa knows better. The bitch was probably scheming to take you the whole time."

Dontae listened as I tried to calm myself.

"You didn't want me, Arianna, let Jaleesa and I be happy. Go find you someone who moves your soul and makes you happy because obviously, I wasn't it. Now if you are done cutting the damn fool, then get the fuck of my office," Dontae spoke aggressively.

I felt as if I was a daze as I stepped out of his office. I pushed through the thick crowd as *(Drake-Fake Love)* blasted. The thick marijuana smoke made my eyes water as I pushed through the double doors to step outside. I gasped for air as the double doors closed behind me. I walked towards my car, slid inside, and burst into tears.

I cried until my head hurt. My heart was broken, I had lost my best friend over some dick. The hurt that I was feeling inside was unimaginable. There was no way in hell I could ever forgive her for the shit she had just done because I knew deep in my heart I could never trust her ever again.

I didn't just cry because I had lost my best friend, but I cried because everything that Dontae had told me had been the truth. I knew that Dontae was a good man and I had completely broken him. Now that he had found someone else to love him and give him what he felt he needed it left me feeling empty inside.

"What now?" I asked myself.

I pulled my car into traffic and headed towards my house. As I cruised through the late-night traffic, thoughts of Dontae and him trying to show me love kept replaying in my mind. The way Dontae had gone over and beyond to try to make me happy I knew he was going to spoil Jaleesa because she was willing to give him what I wouldn't. It was going to be the perfect fairytale with the very man I had abused and treated like shit.

I wiped the tears from my eyes as I pulled up in the driveway. I slid out my car and headed into my house. All of this was about to come to an end, so it was time that I enjoyed my damn self. I headed towards the kitchen and was just about to pour me a drink when I heard footsteps upstairs, followed by a loud crash. Someone was in my fucking house which led me to panic. I grabbed my phone out my purse and hurried to call 911. Just when I was about to tell the operator someone was in my house, someone came from behind and pushed me down on the kitchen floor. My phone fell out my hand and the perpetrator grabbed it. The sound of my phone being smashed is what made me try to make a run for it, but I was too slow. The perpetrator grabbed me roughly and slammed me on the kitchen floor. My whole body was in pain as he dragged me by my hair towards the living room.

The second perpetrator must have heard the commotion because I heard footsteps running down the stairs towards us.

"Looks like the wife of the house has come home in the middle of a robbery," the nigga who attacked me joked under his black ski mask.

His voice sounded like he was a hood ass nigga, but I couldn't make out any of his facial features since he was covered up from head to toe in black.

"Since you are here, you're going to be a good little girl and tell me where your husband keeps his safe at?" The first perpetrator asked.

I shook my head not fully understanding what was going on.

I began to shake and cry, a few moments later the nigga grabbed his gun and pointed it at me.

"Little bitch, where is the fucking safe with the cash in it, if you don't open your mouth and say something, I will have no choice but to blow your fucking brains out."

"Please don't," I cried out.

"Well talk bitch," the dude screamed at me.

"It's upstairs in his office behind the bookshelf," I muttered.

"What's the fucking code?" the second dude asked.

"2465," I cried.

The second perpetrator headed upstairs to retrieve the funds that Dontae kept for hard times while the first perpetrator continued to point his gun at me. It was close to seventy thousand in that fucking safe and now it was going to be all gone. Dontae always made sure that he kept money for a rainy day, but I didn't give a shit about to seventy grand, I just wanted them to let me go.

"You sure fine as hell," the first perpetrator said to me.

The way he was looking at me and rubbing on his dick print made me want to vomit.

"No, don't, please don't do this to me," I cried out to the man as he walked over to me.

"Shut the fuck up bitch, don't fight the shit because I will pull this fucking trigger."

I cried out when he pushed my face down onto the carpet. I heard him unzipping his pants and knew in my heart that there was no escaping this. I laid there as he slid between my legs and slid into me roughing. Tears fell from my eyes, but I accepted that tonight was going to be the night that I died. My life flashed before my eyes as this nigga fucked me from the back. I felt no pain, in fact, I felt numb inside. I had given up on life and had come to terms with God's decision to take me from this fucked up world.

Jaleesa and Dontae flashed before my eyes even though they had betrayed me, there was no point in holding grudges. It was time to let the hurt go.

The sound of the second dude running down the stairs and the moaning and grunting of the dude fucking me let knew that my time was coming to an end.

My body felt weak when the nigga finally slid from off the top of me and zipped his pants back up.

I didn't dare move, instead, I laid there still and began to pray to the man above.

"What the fuck you doing? I can't believe you fucked that girl. This shit better not trace back to us. I got the money, we got to go, I hear sirens," the second preparator said in a panic.

"Nothing is going to get traced back to us if she dead," the first dude spat at his partner.

"Hey, we agreed no one gets hurt."

"Fuck what we said. Give me a quick second to take care of this loose end."

I heard the front door open and then close and then things got quiet.

"I'm sorry to do this to you. You were just at the right place at the wrong fucking time, the dude said just before he took his gun off safety.

"Please don't," I cried.

Pow.

Dontae

I pulled up at the crib to find police cars and the ambulance in my driveway. I parked my car and hopped out to find out what had happened.

"Sir, you can't go in there," a police officer said to me.

"What you mean I can't go in, this is my fucking house, where is my damn wife?" I asked in a panicked voice.

I almost passed out when I spotted Arianna being rolled out in a stretcher.

"What happened?" I cried out.

"Sir, please try to remain calm. We must get her to the hospital she has a gunshot wound to the back of her head." The paramedics told me.

I wasted no time as I hopped back in the ambulance with Arianna. We made it to the hospital in less than ten minutes. I sat in the waiting room and cried my heart out as I waited for someone to tell me something on her condition.

The police from the scene came and sat beside me. He introduced himself as Officer Scott and gave me a little information on what had occurred.

"Your wife called 911, but the call disconnected. Thankfully she stayed on the phone long enough for them to trace her address. It looks like it was a home invasion. Part of the house had been destroyed and we noticed that a safe had been opened. Nothing was inside. It looks like your wife came home in the middle of someone robbing ya'll."

Tears fell down my cheeks as I thought about the pain that Arianna had gone through.

"I have a few questions to ask you."

I nodded my head as I waited on him to ask them.

"Do you know of anyone who would want to hurt your wife?"

"No," I replied sadly.

"Can you tell me where you were at around eleven tonight?"

"I'm the owner of Black Dynasty so I was at the club working."

I watched as the police officer wrote all my contact information down and told me that when they came up with any leads, they were going to let me know.

"Sir, we are doing everything in our power to find out who did this to your wife."

"Thank you."

The officer nodded his head before heading out the door.

I sat in the waiting room close to two hours before a doctor came to introduce himself.

"My name is Dr. Roberts. Are you the husband of Arianna Jordan?"

I stood up and noticed that Dr. Roberts was a black heavy-set man, with thinning hair and wore glasses. He looked like he was around the age of fifty, but I wasn't for us.

"Yes, how is she Doctor?"

The doctor looked at me with gloomy eyes.

"She's in a coma for right now and is in ICU. I stood there in utter disbelief because I couldn't believe what I was hearing. She had one gunshot wound to her head. Far as the bullet, it's still lodged in her brain and she's still in a coma. I honestly don't have no way of learning when she is going to wake up," Dr. Roberts replied sadly.

"Can I see her? I have to see her," I said with tears in my eyes.

The Dr. nodded his head at my request and I slowly followed him towards the ICU. As the door closed behind me, I walked over to where Arianna was laying and stood over her with tears falling from my eyes.

"I'm so sorry I wasn't there for you, please forgive me, baby. Don't leave me, wake up please," I cried out.

The beeping of the machines was all I heard. I took a seat beside her and took a few breaths. I had to call her mother to at least let her know about her daughter.

Ariella picked up her phone on the first ring and all I heard was club music in the background.

"Where in the hell you at? Have you forgotten we were supposed to go over the plans for installing new toilets in the bathrooms?"

"Ariella, I have bad news. I went home and found that Arianna had been shot in the head. I'm at the hospital, she's in ICU."

I heard the screaming and the crying over the phone.

"What room is she in?" Ariella asked emotionally.

I gave her the room number and that's when the call ended.

Ariella was bursting through the doors ten minutes later with tears on her cheek. She looked at me and then to her daughter and cried even harder.

"Why weren't you there to protect her?" Ariella accused me.

I stared at her in disbelief because I didn't want to think this bitch was trying to make it seem like this was my fault.

"I wasn't there with her because I was at fucking club, working, just like you were. The police said that she came home in the middle of us getting robbed."

"I'm sorry if it sounded like I was throwing accusations, I'm just hurt that my only baby, is laid up all because of someone wanting to rob ya'll house."

"Ariella, she's in a coma they don't even know if she is going to wake up."

"The devil is a liar, my daughter is strong. She will beat this I know she will."

I sat there in a trance as Ariella talked to her daughter as if she could hear her.

"Do you think she can hear us?" I asked Ariella.

"I don't know if she can hear us or not, but the best thing to do is talk to her until she finds her way back to us," Ariella replied back.

"Baby, it's your mom, I know you felt as if I was taking control of your life, but I only did these things because I wanted you to have a better life then I did. I wanted you to have the money, power, and material things of this world because I felt this would make you happy, but clearly, I was wrong. It only made you despise me. Please forgive me, baby, come back to me. I promise that I will make this shit right. NO longer will I control your life, but please don't leave me on this Earth all alone. I have only you. You are my only daughter, I can't go on living if you don't," Ariella cried to Arianna motionless body.

I sat there as I listened to Ariella spill her heart to my wife. The buzzing of my cell was what brought me out of the trance that I was in. I pulled my phone out of my pocket and that's when I saw that I had over five text messages from Jaleesa.

I read all five of them before I finally replied to her messages. I had been so consumed with my wife that I had completely forgotten about Jaleesa. There was no better way to tell Jaleesa about Arianna, but once I did, I knew Jaleesa started to panic.

Jaleesa: OMG, is she okay.

Dontae: She was shot in the head. Right now, she's in a coma.

Jaleesa: I can't stop crying. Do I need to come?

Dontae: Come in the morning, Ariella is here and there can only be two people in the room. I don't want to leave her side.

Jaleesa: I understand. See you in the morning.

"Have you told Jaleesa?" Ariella asked as she took a seat beside Arianna.

"I just sent her a message to let her know. She wanted to come, but I told her to wait until morning."

Ariella nodded her head as she stared out the window.

"I know you may think I'm a shitty mother, but I love my daughter."

I didn't respond, I only listened as Ariella began to go deeper.

"Just seeing her laying here and not able to do anything for herself breaks my heart. My daughter didn't deserve this shit."

I wiped the tears that fell from my eyes as I stared at my wife one last time before closing my eyes.

It wasn't long before sleep found me. I didn't know how tired I was until I saw darkness.

It was pitch dark but the glow of the full moon shined inside my bedroom. She pushed me down on the bed before she slid on top of me. her lips on mine made my dick hard and I was eager to slide into her wetness. I groaned as she bit down on my neck as she began to grind on top of me.

"I want you," she whispered into my ear seductively.

"Fuck me like you want me," I told her.

She smiled down at me just as she slid up her black dress. She pulled down my pants and stroked my manhood in her hands. I was rock hard and was ready to please her and she knew this.

I caressed her soft body as she slid on top me. We were connected, we were as one. She looked deep into my eyes as she slowly rode me. She bounced up and down on my wood as I held her by the hips.

Her eyes were closed, and she looked so fucking beautiful and her moans were exquisite. I was near catching my nut when the bedroom door swung open.

The sex fantasy that we were having came to an abrupt end as I spotted Arianna standing there with a pistol in her hand.

"How could you?" Arianna asked with tears in her eyes.

The screams of Jaleesa filled my ears as Arianna pointed the gun at her and then at me.

"Which one is going to go first?" Arianna asked.

"Please don't do this," I begged.

Arianna laughed evilly.

"All these hoes in this world, did you have to fuck my best friend? I didn't care about you leaving me, but leaving me for this bitch, don't sit well with me.

"Arianna please, I'm sorry forgive me."

"It's too late for sorry!" Arianna shouted.

"Pow."

I screamed when Jaleesa head was blown off. Blood splattered the walls and her body fell on top of me.

"You're next," Arianna replied.

"Please, don't."

"Pow."

I woke up to the sound of my phone blasting *Young Thug.*

"Hello," I grumbled into the phone.

"What room are you in?" Jaleesa asked.

I rambled off the number and stood up.

Ariella was already gone, but she had left me a note saying she was going to come back later that day.

I threw the note in the trash, placed a kiss on my wife's forehead before heading into the bathroom to rinse my mouth with mouthwash. A few moments later Jaleesa came in.

She embraced me in a hug before she walked over to Arianna with tears in her eyes.

She grabbed her by her hand and told her how sorry she was. She asked for Arianna's forgiveness which broke my heart. After Jaleesa poured out her heart to Arianna, I watched just to see if Arianna would show some sign that she could hear us, but her status didn't change. I felt nothing but disappointment, but I wasn't going to give up. I was going to keep hope alive. I needed Arianna to wake up, so I could tell her just how sorry I was about everything. I wanted her to know that I never wanted to hurt her intentionally.

Jaleesa walked over to me and grabbed me by the hand. She placed a light kiss on my lips and told me that she was here for me if I needed anything.

"I hate this shit happened to Arianna but at the same time, I want things to go back to how they use to be."

"Nothing will ever be the same anymore. Even if she wakes up, she probably won't be the same Arianna," I told Jaleesa truthfully.

"That's the sad part. The last time I saw her we fought about you. She hated me, it just hurts me to my soul to know that maybe that was my last time seeing her in her normal state."

Jaleesa and I embraced each other in a hug and I held her until she had cried her heart out.

"We were both wrong for betraying her," I told Jaleesa.

"No, we are all grown. She doesn't love you Dontae, you did what any man would do if their own wife didn't want to be with them, you found someone else who adores you." I saw nothing but love in Jaleesa eyes, so I knew that the woman standing in front of me still wanted me, but as I looked back over at Arianna lying helpless in the bed I began to wonder if being with Jaleesa still was a good idea.

Jaleesa must have felt that I was distracted because she took me by the hand and ushered me to leave the room with her. We both got on the elevator and didn't speak to each other until the double doors opened. I followed her outside towards her car and that's when she finally turned around with tears in her eyes.

"You've changed your mind, I can see it in your eyes."

"No, I haven't changed my mind," I said slowly.

"It's just I can't go through with leaving her right now. I mean she's in a coma she's at the lowest right now."

"It doesn't matter baby. It isn't your problem. Why you still loyal to a bitch who doesn't give a fuck about you? She is the only friend I have, and

I said fuck the friendship that we had just so I could be with you, that's just how bad I want you."

I shook my head at her.

"I need more time."

Jaleesa unlocked her car and ushered for me to sit in the passenger seat.

"Let me do something for you to keep your mind at ease and to make sure you don't forget about me."

She didn't even give me time to respond before she zipped down my pants and pulled my manhood out. When her lips wrapped around my dick, that's when all the stress, guilt, and resentment seemed to leave my body and all I felt was lust. I played in her hair as she slurped and played with my dick with her tongue before deep throating me. I could feel the back of her throat as she gave me her all. Slob dripped from my dick as she gagged.

"Fuck," I groaned out.

She pulled her mouth off my dick and lightly stroked my manhood until I reached my peak. As my white cream spilled from out my mushroom dick, Jaleesa licked every drop up with her tongue.

"Damn," was all I could say after she was done.

I zipped my pants up and stared at Jaleesa as she wiped the corner of her mouth.

When she was done cleaning herself up, she looked at me and asked me how long I was going to stay at the hospital.

"I hope you don't plan on being here every day until she wakes up."

I squinted my eyes at Jaleesa.

"Like I said earlier. Arianna needs someone who is going to be here for her at her darkest time. I'm still her husband by law, so I need to be here. I don't want her to wake up and she's alone. I hope you understand."

I could see the hate in Jaleesa eyes, even though her voice told me she understood.

"I have to go."

"Text and call me when you get the chance. Whatever you do, don't forget our plan. Don't let this stop you from your happiness."

I slid out of Jaleesa's car and jogged back towards the hospital. I ordered me something for lunch and had just stepped back into Arianna's room when I noticed the nurses and doctors doing CPR on my wife. I dropped my food to the floor as I stared in horror.

"Sir," one of the nurses called out to me. They grabbed me and ushered me out of the room.

"My wife," I heard myself gasp.

"Let us do our job, everything will be okay," the nurse assured me.

I sat there and prayed that Arianna pulled through, it seemed like it took forever before all the doctors and nurses filed out of her room.

"Will she be okay?" I asked Doctor Roberts when he stepped out.

"She is back stable, so yes, she will be okay," the doctor told me.

I felt as if I was going to pass out, but forced myself to get the overwhelming feeling in check. After the doctor was done talking to me, I headed back into the room with Arianna and closed the door behind myself.

The fear that I just felt took over my whole body.

"Please baby, don't leave me here. Wake up, please," I cried to her.

Jaleesa

A Few Days Later...

It was fucked up what had happened to Arianna. Tears began to roll down my face as I lit me a cigarette. Damn, life could be so fucked up at times, I only hoped that Arianna woke up. I needed her to wake up, so I could tell her just how sorry I was for hurting her. I wanted her to forgive me and I wanted us to go back to how things used to be before I betrayed her.

I bit down on my lip as I wiped the tears from my eyes. Just when I thought that I was going to get Dontae all to myself, that's when this shit happens. When I looked into Dontae eyes, I saw nothing but pain in them. I could still see that he still had deep feelings for Arianna and now that she was in a coma fighting for her life, I knew deep in my heart that the happily ever after was going to be put on hold.

All I wanted was for him to leave her and be with me. I could give him so much but apparently, he didn't want it. I hit my hand up against the steering wheel, every time I remembered him telling me that he couldn't leave Arianna when she was suffering the way she was.

I knew then that he was still in love with her. He still felt as if he was responsible for her when in fact he wasn't. This was his out and he wasn't even trying to take it. I put my cigarette out a few moments later and stepped out my car.

I headed inside the nursing home and clocked in for the night shift. I strolled through the hall in a daze until I heard loud moans nearby. I walked over to the closet where we kept the cleanup materials and placed my ear to the door as the sounds of someone having sex filled my ears. I took a few steps back, grabbed the broom that was standing in the corner, and opened the closet door just so I could see who was in the damn closet fucking.

Every Thursday night, the same shit took place in this fucking closet. I never had the urge to open the closet to see who was fucking in it, I only turned a blind eye to the bullshit, but tonight, I was curious to know the fucking truth. I was tired of turning a blind eye to what was happening around me.

I stood there in utter disbelief when I spotted my supervisor and one of the most popular doctors fucking.

I slammed the door and hurried to do my rounds. I wanted to unsee what I had seen, but it was too late for all that. Just thinking that the bitch who had given me hell since I had first started working here was fucking one of the doctors still had me shook. The bitch always pressed the issue on how we should conduct ourselves at work and was quick to fire anyone who didn't do what she said and here she was doing the unthinkable.

My supervisor was in her late thirties and she felt she was the Queen of the fucking facility. She had a big ass ego and was always trying to make an example of someone. Now that I knew what she did every Thursday night I was ready for her to come with me on some bullshit, I'm sure the doctor she was fucking wife would be very interested in learning what her husband was doing while she was laying home pregnant with their third child. Niggas weren't shit and neither was these dumb ass hoes.

After I had made my rounds only then did I pull out my phone and try to call Dontae.

My body went stiff when he sent my call to voicemail.

I called his ass back and yet again he ignored my call.

I put my phone in my pocket and tried to calm myself down. He was going through a hard time, I needed to give him time and space to come to terms with things. Even though he didn't want to leave his wife he was going to eventually have to give her up, especially if she didn't wake from her coma.

I took a few deep breaths, headed into the bathroom, splashed water over my face so I could pull myself together. I stared at myself in the mirror and saw nothing in them. My eyes were empty and I guess it was because I felt numb inside.

I was just about to walk out of the bathroom to get back to work when my supervisor walked into the bathroom. The nastiness that she normally had towards me had totally evaporated.

"Can we talk for a quick minute?" she asked.

I didn't speak, I only waited on her to continue what she had to say.

"What you saw back there, can't get back to his wife or anyone, I know. I have acted like a bitch towards you, but I need you to keep what you just seen to yourself. It will ruin him and myself," my supervisor responded.

When she was done, I looked at her for the longest moment before telling her that her secret was safe with me.

"Thank you, Jaleesa, a lead position is coming available next month, if you put an application in, the position is yours."

"Sounds like a deal," I told her before I walked out of the bathroom.

If the bitch wanted to keep me quiet by boosting my pay and giving me a lead position, then I was going to take her up on that offer. I was tired of cleaning up shit and vomit, I deserved more then what I was putting in.

The rest of the night I walked the halls and checked on all my patients that I had been assigned to for that night. I tried my hardest to not think of Dontae and the plans of us being together. I also thought of Arianna and how our friendship was in shambles. I had made a fucking mess of shit, I only prayed that when Arianna woke up that things were where they needed to be.

After clocking out of work, I didn't go home to sleep like I normally did. Instead, I pulled up at Dontae's crib to find that his car was parked outside. I knocked on his door and he answered a few moments later.

"What are you doing here?" Dontae asked.

He was dressed in a pair of basketball shorts and a plain red shirt. He looked as if he hadn't slept in days. His dreads needed to be retwisted and he had bags under his eyes.

Instead of answering his question I pushed past him and headed towards the kitchen to pour me a glass of wine.

"I called you last night while I was at work and you ignored both of my calls. What I'm not going to allow to happen is let you throw me away like I'm some fucking trash. We had plans and you trying to go back on them."

"Don't you see what just happened to my wife?"

"Oh, so now she's your wife now. She wasn't your wife when you were fucking me in your office and telling me that you were ready to leave her to be with me. She wasn't your fucking wife when I was sucking your dick in my car outside the fucking hospital."

"Will you please fucking stop, I don't know what to fucking do!" Dontae yelled.

I slammed my glass of wine down and walked over to him.

"Leave her Dontae like you told me that you would. You know whenever she wakes up the bitch ain't going to be bothered by thanking you for being there for her. She going to sign the divorce papers as soon as the bitch can write her name. Be a fucking man and do what is needed to be done," I spat at him.

"I can't, I know Arianna have her issues, and I know how she feels about me, but she was shot in the head. She is going to need me. Leaving her when she needs me the most will be fucked up."

I took a few steps back and shook my head at him.

"I know she may hate me when she gets up, but she will eventually see things clearly. Yes, I fucked up by fucking around with her ex, but technically you aren't her ex if she never loved you."

I could tell that I had hurt Dontae's feelings, but I was tired of playing games with him, either he was going to be with me or he wasn't.

I held my breath as he walked over to me and caressed my face.

"Jaleesa, I care about you, that night when we fucked. I was weak and angry that I was giving Arianna so much love and she didn't seem to want it. When you came to me and saw the pain that I was in and promised that you could give me what she couldn't, I wanted that at the time. I needed to hear everything that you had said, I was willing to do the unthinkable and leave her, but after coming home to find that she was shot in the head from a robbery gone wrong, really fucked my head up. The guilt that I feel inside is so fucking strong. We both betrayed her Jaleesa, all I want to do is make things right. When she wakes up, I want to do my part to make sure she is okay."

I pulled away from him.

"So basically, you are telling me you changed your mind about me and you?"

Dontae became quiet as if he was in deep thought.

"Never mind, it took you to fucking long to answer that question."

I was heading out the door when he yelled out my name.

I stopped and turned around to face him.

"Please, understand," he pleaded.

I chuckled.

"I understand that you hate yourself to the point of torturing yourself. Who stays in a marriage when the other person tells you directly, they don't want you or will ever love you? Whatever she puts you through you deserve the shit."

He was just about to respond but I didn't give his ass the time to. I slammed the door behind myself and hopped into my car. Tears fell from my eyes as I pulled out his driveway. My blurred vision almost caused me to have a head-on collision.

I was driving not really knowing where I was going. I pulled up at the hospital a few moments later and sat in the car for the longest. I lit me a cigarette and tried to calm myself down before I headed inside.

When I reached Arianna's room, the smell of flowers filled my nose. I walked over to her and took a seat by her bed. I grabbed her hand and began to talk to her. I poured out my heart out to her because deep down I knew this was probably going to be my last time ever seeing her.

"Arianna, this Jaleesa, I don't know if you can hear me or not but if you can, please just listen. I know you may hate me about what I have done to you, but I just want you to forgive me. All I ever wanted was to be happy, I thought I was going to have that with Dontae, but I was completely wrong. Even though he knows how you feel about him he still wants to remain by your side. Crazy huh? I know."

I laughed.

I wiped my nose with a piece of tissue that I grabbed off the table beside me and kept on talking.

"I fucked up our friendship, I admit I did. I only was thinking of myself. I felt as if I was doing us both a favor. You didn't want to be married and I wanted everything that you had. The fact you didn't have any love for Dontae was the only reason why I went after him as I did. If you would have loved him, never would I have ever done something like this? I thought he was just some piece of trash you didn't want. When you attacked me the way you did, really opened my eyes to some painful shit. I was still wrong, for going after what was yours, and I'm sorry about that. I've tried to persuade him to leave you, but now that you are laid up in here fighting for your life, he has made it clear that he will never leave you until you open your eyes, and even then, he's going to remain by your side to make sure that you're okay. The plan of him divorcing you is no longer happening, so with that being said, there is no use for me to be here any longer. I pray that you wake up and you be okay. My heart is broken, but it's time for me to let things go. I'm tired of fighting for shit and coming up empty-handed. All I wanted was Dontae and even he turned his back on me," I cried.

I squeezed her hand just before I stood up.

"If and when you wake up, don't come looking for me because you won't be able to find me. I love you Arianna and I'm sorry for everything."

I rubbed my hands through her tangled her and was just about to leave when the doctor stepped inside.

"Have there been any changes?"

"Sadly, no. But let's not give up. She still has a twenty-five percent chance of waking up. Just keep hope alive."

"I'm sorry doctor, but I have no hope left in me," I whispered.

I walked out of the hospital and I ran smack into Dontae. I didn't even bother by speaking to him. I just kept on walking as if he was just a stranger on the street. He called out for me, but I ignored his calls. I

hopped back into my car and headed home.

Dontae

Some Days Later...

I sat down in utter disbelief as I stared back at the same police officer who I spoke to the night that Arianna was found.

"Mr. Jordan, I do want to inform you that when Arianna was brought in for her gunshot wound a rape kit was performed on her as well. Most attacks this brutal are sometimes sexual attacks as well."

When Officer Scott told me that Arianna had been raped, I was numb inside. A tear fell from my eyes as I grabbed Arianna by her hand.

"We ran the DNA into the database, and we found the suspect who committed the rape. Right now, we have him downtown and is questioning him. My partner who is helping me work this case told me that he didn't act alone. He had an accomplice with him. I assure you, Mr. Jordan, we have enough evidence to put both away from a very long time."

I didn't trust myself to speak, all I could do was nod my head at him.

After Officer Scott had left out the room, I turned and gave Arianna my full attention.

"I hope you got a chance to hear what the police officer said, they said they found the suspects who did this to you and they have enough to send them both away for a very long time. Baby, if you can hear me, please just let me know that you are there."

Tears fell from my eyes, but Arianna made no attempt to let me know that she had heard anything. Was I really wasting my time coming to see her every day only to be let down? I thought that maybe if she knew she was loved that she would wake up, but still she laid there stiff.

I wiped the last bit of my tears from my eyes and stood up from the chair. Even though part of me wanted to give up on her, the other part told me to hang on just a little while longer. I was just about to head into the cafeteria to get me some lunch when I bumped into Ariella.

"How my baby doing? Has she shown any improvements?"

"Nothing."

I could see the stress behind her eyes and I took that time to embrace her in a hug. Since Arianna had been in the coma, I made sure that Ariella was the one who oversaw of the running of the club due to the fact, I wasn't in the right mindset to do it. Ariella went to work every single day and gave me the rundown on what was happening.

"I'm going to head up there to see her, stay here, and enjoy your food. You look like you haven't eaten in days or slept."

"I just can't stop thinking about what happened."

"It's going to be okay. Arianna's a fighter, she's going to pull through this."

"I just don't know Ariella."

Ariella was just about to walk away when I grabbed her by her arm.

"I just talked to the police officer, he came by to give me some news on Arianna's case."

Ariella stood there and waited eagerly for me to tell her what I knew.

"Officer Scott told me that Arianna was raped. They pulled some DNA when she was first brought in and it came back as a positive match to someone. Officer Scott said that him and his partner have enough evidence to send over to the DA and get him put away for a long time."

"My baby was raped?" Ariella cried.

I grabbed her and embraced her in a tight hug as she cried.

"The one who raped her told police that he wasn't along, and he had an accomplice with him as well."

"I hope neither one of them get out of jail."

Ariella pulled away from me and fixed her clothes just before she headed towards Arianna's room.

I entered the half-empty cafeteria and grabbed me a chicken sandwich, a large sweet tea, and fries before I headed to the register to pay for my items. I took a seat in a chair and opened my food slowly. I took a few bites before I pushed my food away. Thoughts of Jaleesa began to hunt me. I had hurt her and it wasn't my intention to do any of that. I wanted to make things right with her, but what Jaleesa wanted there was no way that I could give it to her right now. I had already made my decision to be there for my wife instead of running off with her. I was willing to give up on love just so I could do my duties as a husband and be there for my wife. I took my vows to Arianna serious, I was going to be there with her through sickness and death, I wasn't going to leave her side until I knew she was going to be okay.

I took a few sips of my drink before getting up and throwing my food away. I was just about to walk out of the cafeteria to head back up to Arianna's room when I noticed a young couple sitting down eating lunch. I overheard them talking about getting married. My heart felt heavy as I walked past them. They were both in love, I could see how they were looking at one another. Now I understood what Arianna had been stressing to me for so many months. Arianna didn't look at me like this young girl was looking at the man she was due to marry soon.

I pushed the couple from my mind and headed up the elevator back towards Arianna's room. Ariella was still there holding her hand and whispering something to her. Ariella became quiet when she saw me walk in.

"You finished eating that fast?" Ariella asked.

"I wasn't really hungry."

Ariella walked over to me and placed a kiss on my cheek.

"I know you're going through a lot emotionally, but you have to eat and take care of yourself. When my baby wakes up, you need to be in your right frame of mind. Go home get some damn sleep, shower, and come back later if you want. I will sit with her until you get back."

I tried to put up a fight, but all the energy that I was feeling inside felt depleted. I walked out of the hospital and headed home. I pulled up at my house and sat in the car for the longest time as I tried to calm myself down. I began to question and wonder if I was even doing the right thing.

I pulled out my phone and had the urge to call Jaleesa, but my heart wouldn't allow me to do it. I sighed as I stepped out my car and made my way into my house. I didn't even make it to the bed, instead I fell on the couch and fell into a deep sleep.

Soft hands caressed my face and her words seemed to comfort my soul.

"I love you, come be with me," Jaleesa called out to me.

I looked around me but couldn't see Jaleesa at first. A few moments later I spotted her floating from the ocean water. The sun was setting, and it was going to be nightfall soon.

She held her hand out to me, to try to get me to follow her into the water, but my feet remained firmly on the sandy beach.

"Why are you so afraid? Don't you want to be loved the right way?" she asked me with a pleading face.

"All I ever want is to be loved," I heard myself reply.

"I can give you all the love in the world if you just come to me."

Even though I felt as if I was in a frozen state, I managed to start to move my feet. I stepped into the cold water and made my way towards her, I felt as if I was in a trance because her beauty was something that I couldn't resist. As the sun radiated off her caramel skin, I felt a sudden warmness wash over me. I felt as if things were going to be okay. Just when I was almost close enough to touch her, was when I was jerked awake from the sound of someone beating down my front door.

I took a few moments to stretch before I made my way to the door to find out who it was. My heart began to race when I spotted Officer Scott standing on my front porch. I took a deep breath and let him in. He looked around my living room before taking a seat on my couch, he glared at me and I saw nothing but sympathy in his eyes.

"How are you holding up?" Officer Scott asked with concern.

"I'm barely making it. As you can see when this shit happened to my wife, my whole life stopped."

Officer Scott dropped two pictures of two men on my coffee table before training his eyes on me.

"These are the two men who robbed your house. Do you know these two guys?"

I took a good look at both black niggas who had ruined my life but neither one of them looked familiar.

"I came over here to inform you that the one that raped your wife hung himself in prison this morning. The second one is still alive and will be facing charges from the DA. We have mounting of evidence, so we are confident that this will be a win. He will remain in jail, no bond until his trial. I will make sure to keep you up to date on what happens with him."

I stood there frozen as I placed both pictures of the two niggas back on the table. I was pissed inside that the one who had caused the pain of hurting my wife had taken the easy way out.

A few tears fell from my eyes and I hurried to wipe them away.

"Mr. Jordan, we are doing everything we can to get justice for this matter."

"Thanks, Officer," I choked out.

I walked him to the door to let him out, after he had slid back into his patrol car only then did, I lose all sense of control. I slammed the front door behind myself and started trashing my living room. After I had gotten all the anger that I was feeling inside out, I looked at the mess that I had just made.

Vases were smashed, pillows were thrown to the floor the two sofas were flipped over, the T.V had been smashed, and even the wall art that I had spent thousands on had gotten torn up. I headed upstairs towards the bathroom and hopped in the shower. I washed the grime and sweat off my body and washed my dreads before stepping out. I stared at myself in the mirror and saw nothing but pain in my eyes. A nigga was hurting, and I felt lost. I took care of my hygiene and made sure to dry my dreads before I put on some clean clothes. After I had gotten dressed, I grabbed my keys and headed back to the hospital. The life that I once had was now gone. I was at the hospital so much I was beginning to think I lived there my damn self.

A few minutes later, I pulled up at my usual spot and headed inside. As soon as I stepped on the ICU floor, every woman on that floor stared at me which was irritating to me. A few of them I knew wanted to fuck and I knew that by how they couldn't take their eyes off me. Even though I was a sexy as nigga and could pull any bitch that I wanted, right now wasn't the time for any of this. A bitch was the last thing on my mind. When I pushed open Ariana's door, I spotted a nurse standing over her, and checking her to make sure she was okay.

"Have there been any change?" I asked the nurse.

The nurse was a young black girl with long thick hair that was pulled up in a bun on top of her head. She had a pretty face and the look of innocence about her. She didn't speak, she only shook her head no before walking out.

After the door had closed behind her, I walked over to Arianna and began to caress her hand.

"I'm here for you Arianna, its safe for you to wake up. You have been sleeping for two weeks. I don't know how much I can take. I'm literally losing all sense of myself. If you can hear me, please baby wake up," I cried out to her.

I laid my head on her stomach as I cried to her.

A few moments later, I felt something move under me. I stood there for a few seconds believing that I had seriously lost my mind. She had laid stiff in this bed it seemed forever with no improvement. I pulled away from her and that's when I felt her hand squeeze my own. Arianna was finally awake. All the crying and pleading had been heard. I pushed the button on her bed to let the nurses and the doctors know that Arianna was trying to wake up.

Her eyes began to flutter and my anxiety level shot up to the roof. When her eyes finally opened, I knew that things were going to be okay.

Arianna

The voice of Dontae pleading to me sounded so far away. I had no way of reaching him and I felt as if we were in different worlds. The harder that I tried to get to him the more it seemed that I was pushed farther away from him. Instead of fighting this, I decided to surrender. The sound of loud beeping filled my ears as my eyes began to open. The bright light was painful to my eyes and my vision was blurry. I groaned in pain and tried to sit up, but I couldn't, I felt as if I was frozen into place. I was beginning to panic because I had no clue where I was at or what was going on. I mean why in the fuck couldn't I move?

"Mrs. Jordan, please remain calm, you're in the hospital. You're safe now."

I blinked my eyes a few times just, so my vision would clear up. I could hear someone talking to me, but I couldn't make out exactly who they were or how they looked. I took a few deep breaths and tried to calm my own self down.

I reopened my eyes and was grateful that my vision was finally clearer. There were close to five nurses and two doctors standing around me. They were checking my vitals and writing shit down on a clipboard as they observed me.

"My name is Dr. Roberts, I have been your doctor since you came in two weeks ago."

"What?" I asked in confusion.

"Can you tell me your name?"

My name is Arianna Jordan," I replied hoarsely.

"Can you tell me who the president of the United States?"

I squinted my eyes at him before replying, "Donald Trump."

"Can you tell me the last thing remember?"

"I can't think right, my head is killing me," I whined.

The Doctor signaled for the nurse to give me morphine before instructing me to relax.

As the nurses left out the room the Doctor remained, but he wasn't along. I glanced across the room and that's when I spotted Dontae talking to the Doctor in the far side of the corner. They were whispering something to one another.

"Dontae," I said hoarsely.

Dontae stopped what he was doing and walked over to me.

He had tears in his eyes as he bent down and placed a gentle kiss on my lips.

"Shhhhh, don't talk baby. Let me go get you a drink of water."

I didn't want him to leave me in and began to cry out for him to stay.

"I'm just going down the hall, I will be right back."

I tried reaching out to him, but my arms had no strength to them. As the morphine began to kick in, I began to become super relaxed.

"Dr. Roberts, I don't want any more morphine, I don't want to go back to sleep," I began to cry.

"Relax Mrs. Jordan, the morphine is only relaxing your body, nothing more."

A few moments later Dontae came back with a small paper cup of water. He tried passing the cup to me, but I couldn't even take it. My body was just that weak.

Tears fell down my cheeks as Dontae instructed me to open my mouth.

"Don't cry sweetie, I'm going to help you through this."

As the cool water penetrated my throat, flashbacks of what I last remember began to resurface of Dontae and me, things were all beginning to come together. After the water was gone, Dontae took a seat next to me as he continued to talk to the Doctor about my recovery process.

"As you may know, your wife has been in a comatose state for two weeks. The next step is to evaluate her to see how much she can remember and also how long it is going to take her to recover physically."

"I remember you cheated on me with my best friend," I interrupted their conversation.

Dontae grew stiff and that's when I knew without a doubt that the visions that I had were correct.

"Do tell more," the doctor replied.

I stared at Dontae and started from the beginning of that awful night.

"I went to the club because I had just found out that you were sleeping with my best friend, I was upset and hysterical. I felt betrayed by you both. I left out of your office angry that you was going to divorce me to be with her. Even though I pushed you in her direction by treating you like shit and telling you that I couldn't love you and didn't want to love you, I still felt that you were mine. I didn't want ya'll together. I was being selfish, I felt like there were so many women out there that could love you, why did you have to take my best friend away from me? So, I left to go home, I walked into my house and went into my kitchen. That's when I heard something upstairs, like footsteps. I knew that I wasn't alone because I had just left you at the club. No one had a key to our house, so I began to panic and called 911 only for the phone to be snatched out my hand. I was pushed to the floor and dragged into the living room."

Tears began to fall from my eyes as the memories began to come back even stronger.

"The man had a gun pointed to me and…"

Dontae head dropped.

"Do you remember anything that happened after that?"

I nodded my head slowly.

"He sexually assaulted me while his other partner was upstairs getting the money out the safe. I knew that I was going to die and all I wanted to do before I took my last breath was to forgive you and my best friend. My last wish was for both of you to be happy. I didn't want to die with hate in my heart for either one of ya'll. After the dude finished sexually assaulting me, he pointed the gun at me. I begged for my life, but he said he couldn't spare me. The last thing I remember is the sound of the gun going off and I saw nothing but darkness."

The doctor stared at me for the longest time before he spoke.

"You went through a terrible ordeal and I'm glad to say that your memory is still in place. Most wake up and don't remember their names or where they're from or the year that we are in. The longer you are in a comatose sleep the greater the damage towards brain activity. All we must do now is get you where you are physically able to do things on your own. This may take a little time, but you will be going home before you know it."

"Nooo, I can't stay here, I don't want to be here, I want to go home."

"Mrs. Jordan, you're not yet physically ready to go home right now."

I began to cry and that's when Dontae squeezed my hand and told me that things were going to be okay.

"You have to listen to the doctor sweetie."

"I just want to go home," I cried.

"We will be moving you from ICU later today to a regular room. Tomorrow we will start bright and early for your physical and motor treatments."

"Thank you, Doctor Roberts, for all you have done," Dontae said gratefully.

After the doctor had walked out of the room I looked over at Dontae. My heart began to ache for him because I could remember him talking to me so fucking much when I was asleep. He was the one who kept me alive with hope that one day I was going to wake back up.

"You need to rest Dontae, you have been here since I've been here. I heard everything that you, my mother, and Jaleesa said to me. Even though I couldn't respond, I still heard ya'll. Honestly, you were the only one that kept me going, I believe if you would have stopped coming to see me, I feel like I would have died eventually. I felt loved the whole time that I was in that coma."

"Arianna, you are loved. I promised you that I wasn't going to leave and I'm still not going to leave you. I want to make sure that you are fully healed and able to do things for yourself again."

"And after I'm fully myself, are you going to take off with Jaleesa?" I asked him sadly.

Dontae became silent.

"Arianna, Jaleesa and I were both wrong for going behind your back and trying to be together. At the time it felt like the right thing to do, she honestly care about me, and she is willing to give me exactly what I couldn't get from you. The fact that you said you never loved me made me feel like the lowest piece of scum on Earth. I wanted someone to give my all to and who was going to appreciate me. We honestly thought you wouldn't care since you didn't want me anyway."

I began to cry silently, and Dontae walked over and held me in his arms.

"Shhhhh, don't cry. I did the right thing. I broke it off with Jaleesa, a few days ago."

I pulled away from him.

"I already know that."

Dontae stared at me with a confused look on his face.

"She came to me and told me everything. Where is she now? She told me not to look for her when I woke up."

"I haven't heard from her. She left me alone after I told her I had to be here to make sure you were going to be okay. I couldn't run away with her and forget the promise that I had made to you. I didn't care how bad you had hurt me, you needed me, and I didn't want to forsake you."

"I don't know what I've done to deserve such a good man. I'm so sorry for everything," I cried to him.

Dontae was just about to speak when a knock came at the door.

We both glanced up and that's when I spotted my mother, with a vase of flowers in her hand.

"Baby, you're awake," my mother cried.

Dontae grabbed the vase of flowers and sat them on the nightstand beside my bed as my mother placed a kiss on my forehead.

"I'm so glad that you finally woke up, I've missed you so much. My life had no meaning when you weren't here."

I stared at her and that's when I noticed she was crying real tears.

"Baby, I know I haven't always been the best mother to you, but I do want you to know that I love you so fucking much. I'm so thankful that the Lord didn't take you away from me before I told you how I felt about you. From this day forward, I'm going to be all about my daughter. For the rest of my days, I want to make things right between us, no more hate and animosity."

My mom wiped my tears away as her and I lightly talked about things. Dontae only observed us from a distance, I guess he just wasn't in the mood to talk or interrupt our girl time. My mother and I talked until it was dinner time. When they brought out my tray of food, my mother stood up to kiss me goodbye.

"Baby, I will come back and see you tomorrow, I have to go get things situated at the club for tonight. Dontae has been here watching over you since you first came. So, you won't have to worry about being here alone," my mother said as she headed out the door.

After my mother had gone, Dontae took a seat beside me.

"Are you hungry?" Dontae asked me.

"Yes."

Dontae grabbed my fork from off my tray and handed it to me.

"Let's see what all you can do."

The smell of green beans, pork chops, and roll, filled my nostrils. My stomach growled which made Dontae laugh.

I held the fork with shaky hands but that was all I could do. The harder I tried to pick up my green beans the more my hands shook. My motor skills were off point which was frustrating to me.

Tears fell from my eyes and Dontae wiped them away.

"Don't cry."

"I can't even fucking feed myself," I cried to him.

"Arianna, you been in a deep sleep for two weeks, it's going to take time for your body to adjust. Give it time, things will go back to normal soon. Open your mouth and I will feed you myself."

I did as I was told. After Dontae had fed me my food, he grabbed my water off the tray and made sure that I drunk all of it.

"Thank you."

"Your welcome," he replied.

I watched him as he sat everything on the tray and pushed it away from my body.

"Do you need me to help you go to the bathroom or are you okay?"

"I'm okay. I don't need to go right now."

"Well, whenever you do, just let me know."

"Dontae, have you told Jaleesa, that I'm awake?"

Dontae was just about to speak when the nurses came in and told me that they finally had my room ready for me. The nurses pulled the covers from over my body and helped me into a wheelchair. We headed towards the elevator and had just stepped inside when I spotted Jaleesa staring at me.

"Jaleesa?" I called out to her, but it was too late, the elevator doors had slammed shut.

"Dontae can you tell her what room, I'm going to be in."

Dontae pulled out his phone and sent her a text as the elevator doors swooshed open again. My heart began to race because I didn't know what to expect when I saw her again. The last time we had been in each other presence I had chocked her ass out, but this time it wasn't going to be anything like that. I wanted nothing but peace.

After I had been directed into my room and had gotten comfortable that's when Jaleesa walked in. She was dressed in plain clothes and her hazel green eyes looked swollen as if she had been crying. She walked over to where I was sitting and took a seat next to the bed.

Dontae quickly excused himself which I was grateful for. It was time that Jaleesa and I got the chance to get some things straight between us.

I cleared my throat and was just about to get ready to tell her how I felt when she stopped me.

"I'm glad that you're awake, I came by to see you, I don't know if you heard any of the things that I said to you, but..."

"Jaleesa, stop right there. I have something to say to you. You are my best friend and when I found out that you had slept with my husband I freaked out."

"But you don't love him..."

"No, I didn't love him right then. I wanted out of my marriage and was willing to do anything just to be free from it all. Even though my mother was trying to make sure that both of our bags was secured for the future, I was unhappy. I didn't see all the things that Dontae was doing for me, I didn't see the sacrifices that he made every day. I didn't see what we could be if I could just open my eyes and see him for who he truly was. Tears fell from my eyes as I stared at her.

I couldn't love him then, I didn't want to, but when you came to me and told me that you were going to take him off my hands, every inch of me began to hurt, I felt betrayed I was angry, because never do we ever go after each other ex's."

"Arianna, even though he was your ex legally, you didn't have the bond or the love for him to be your ex romantically. I understand that neither one of us went behind one another and fucked with anyone who we romantically loved, but I felt Dontae was fair game since you didn't have any type of love towards him. I thought that maybe I was doing you a favor. Dontae is everything that I ever wanted. He has so much love in his heart and he can also give me the financial security that I have always prayed for."

I wiped the tears from my eyes before I stared at Jaleesa for the longest time.

"Jaleesa, it's something that you must know that will change everything. When I walked in on the two men robbing my house, never did I ever imagine that I would end up here, but here I am. Do you know while I was being sexually assaulted, you and Dontae were all I thought about? I wanted to forgive you both and I wanted both of ya'll happy. If Dontae was happy with you then I was going to stay out of it, all I wanted before I died was to die without holding a grudge and no hate in my heart. I promised myself that if I survived that night, I was going to make things right with the both of you. I just want you to know that I love you Jaleesa and always will, but you can't have my husband. It took me to nearly die for the love in my heart to finally awaken inside of me. When I woke up today, he was here. He came and talked to me every single day, I felt he was the reason why I stayed strong and didn't fade away to nothingness."

I could see the anger in Jaleesa eyes, but she didn't speak at first instead she only stared at me as if she was in a trance, and then all of a sudden, she laughed.

She stood up and stared down at me.

"I don't know or understand why Dontae can't let you go. I tried persuading him to leave your ass in here to rot and decay, but he wasn't having any of that shit, he was determined to stay by your side until the very end. I'm not going to lie, I'm hurt and jealous of the love that he has for you, and I'm pissed that someone as selfish as you can even keep a man like him. You claim that you have finally opened up your heart to your husband after this tragic accident, I wonder how long this is going to last? You're just being sentimental right now, with the gunshot to the head and all. You aren't thinking clearly. You don't really want Dontae, you just don't want him to leave you alone in this fucking hospital. You don't even deserve his loyalty."

"Get the fuck out of my damn room. The hate that you have for me is fucking sickening. You have ruined my fucking life, you know deep down you don't want Dontae, it's all for the moment, but instead of setting him free, you rather use him until he can't be used anymore."

"Get out!" I yelled.

Jaleesa shook her head at me. She smiled wickedly as a few tears fell down her cheeks.

"I want Dontae so bad, I deserve him," she cried.

"You may want him, but he will never be yours," replied maliciously.

Jaleesa looked at me like I had just punched her ass.

"Goodbye," Arianna she muttered under her breath before she headed out the door.

𝒟𝑜𝓃𝓉𝒶𝑒

Instead of hanging around Arianna's room, I decided the best thing to do was to give Jaleesa and her enough time to talk shit out and make things right between them. I stuck a dollar into the vending machine and grabbed me a Sprite to drink. As I sipped on my drink, I walked towards the sitting area and took a seat. I pulled out my phone and hit my mother in law up.

"Hey Arielle, I just wanted to call to see how things going at the club."

"Things are going well. There is going to be a big ass party tonight so we going to get three times what we normally make."

"Cool, I see you have everything handled."

"Of course, you know I'm going to keep things flowing. This is our income, no time for fuck ups."

"I'm grateful I have you in my corner. Remember you were telling me how you wanted to remodel the bathrooms? I just wanted to let you know that you can whatever you feel like needs to be done."

"I'm glad to hear that, I will get on it asap. You don't need to be stressing over anything, just take care of my daughter, she needs you. How are things going with her?"

"They just moved her to a new room, she's in there talking with Jaleesa now."

I didn't both by telling her all the shit that had been going on with Jaleesa, Arianna and I. I didn't want to cause any more drama then I already had. If Arianna hasn't told her shit that meant I wasn't about to speak on the shit.

After I ended the call with Arielle, I headed back to Arianna's room to find her sitting in the bed crying.

"Baby, you okay?" I asked her.

"Jaleesa and I got into it again."

She rubbed her hands through her tangled hair and sighed with frustration.

"Our friendship is over."

"I'm sorry baby, I know I fucked all this up for you."

She shook her head at me.

"No, you didn't fuck it up."

"She wants you, always wanted you. So, this was bound to happen

eventually."

"I just hate it had to come to this."

I walked over to her and wiped her tears from her eyes.

"Things are going to get better," I promise.

"Dontae, I have something to tell you."

My heart began to beat erratically as I waited to see what she had to say.

"I just want to say thanks for being here for me. Most men would have

left my ass long ago, but you didn't. I know I've acted so cold to you and

I'm sorry about that. I just want to make things right with us, I want to do

right by you. You deserve so fucking much. I never thought I would be

saying this shit, but here I am, sitting here barely able to do anything for

myself and of all people you are here with me. I never thought I could love

you, but it took me to nearly die to finally open my heart to you. When

Jaleesa told me how much she wanted you for herself, it pained my heart

because I was finally awake. I finally see what she has been saying from

day one. I finally understand what she means about how good you truly are. There is no way in hell I want to give my marriage up. I can't let you go, I can't let you walk out of my life. I need you and I have nothing but love and respect for you. All I ask is that you forgive me and we start over."

My heart felt heavy because I had been waiting so long to hear her say these words. I caressed her cheek with my finger before placing my lips on hers. She slid her tongue into my mouth and our tongues danced together. I felt the love radiating off her body and it filled the void that was in my heart.

I pulled away from her and looked deeply into her eyes. I love you Arianna and I forgive you.

I grabbed a comb from out my overnight bag and started to untangle her hair. We talked and laughed with one another as I combed her hair back into a ponytail. I placed a kiss on her forehead when I was done.

"You look beautiful."

"I bet I look a hot ass mess but thank you."

I chuckled.

"Even though you're rocking a hospital gown you still look good enough to eat."

Arianna smirked at me.

"Can you help me up, I have to go to the bathroom."

I pulled the covers from over her body and helped her out the bed.

"Do you think you can walk?"

"I don't know, I'm going to try."

I watched as Arianna placed her hands on the bed as she tried to steady herself. Just when she thought she could let herself go that's when she almost fell. I grabbed her and helped her the rest of the way to the bathroom.

"I hate this shit, I can't even walk," she cried.

"You will get your strength back, but it isn't going to happen overnight."

I helped her sit on the toilet and watched her to make sure she didn't fall. When she was done using the bathroom, I grabbed some tissue and made sure to clean her. I helped her off the toilet and walked her back to her bed a few moments later.

I had just put her back in the bed when Dr. Roberts knocked on the door.

"Physical therapy will be first thing in the morning. Get some rest tonight because tomorrow the goal is to start the process of you recovering." Dr. Roberts informed Arianna.

"Thanks, Dr. Roberts." Arianna told me.

After he had left out of the room, I flipped to a movie on Lifetime and watched it with Arianna until she finally fell into a deep sleep. I placed a kiss on her lips and walked over to the chair that I normally slept at and closed my eyes as well.

∞∞∞∞

The Next Morning

After I had fed Arianna her breakfast, the nurse came into the room with a wheelchair.

"Are you ready?" the nurse asked Arianna nicely.

"I'm ready," Arianna replied as the nurse helped her in the wheelchair.

When we stepped into the fitness room, the nurse told us that someone else was on the way to take care of Arianna. After the doors closed and the nurse was out of sight, I bent down so I could have a talk with Arianna.

"All I want you to do is do the best you can do. This isn't going to be a fast process so try to remain calm and do everything that the nurse and doctor says."

She grabbed me tightly and asked if I was going to stay with her.

"Of course, I am. I'm not leaving your side."

The door swung open a few moments later and in walked Dr. Roberts with one of his nurses.

I watched her for over an hour as my wife tried to learn how to walk all back over again. I didn't take my eyes off her not once.

When she started to cry, I walked over her to her and whispered encouraging words in her ear.

When the session was over, the nurse helped her back into her wheelchair and Dr. Roberts gave me the run down on her progress.

"Arianna did great today. I have confidence that she will recover rather fast. She wasn't in a coma long, so she will be going home sooner than we originally thought."

"Are you sure Doctor?"

"I know it may look bad now, but I have seen worst. So yes, I give it another two weeks and she will be her old self again. Her body was laying still for a short amount of time than the patients that I worked with previously," the doctor assured me.

After Dr. Roberts and the nurse had left, I grabbed her wheelchair and told her the good news. This seemed to brighten her mood.

"Baby, all you need to do is work your muscles as much as you can."

"No more babying you and feeding you. We going to try something different today."

"I agree," Arianna told me as I pushed her back into her room.

I helped her out of her wheelchair and watched as she grabbed the bed for support. She slowly slid herself into the bed and I placed the sheets over her.

"You already doing better, just yesterday you couldn't even get into bed by yourself."

Arianna smiled at me.

"You're so right, I'm getting better, I'm making progress, that's all I care about."

"Good," I told her.

I cut on the T.V and put it on mute. We talked for a little while before the nurses brought the trays out for lunch.

The smell of spaghetti and meatballs filled the room.

"Are you ready to eat?" I asked her.

"Ugh, I'm so sick and tired of this hospital food."

I chuckled.

"You won't be eating this shit for much longer."

"I hope not because this food tastes like death."

We both laughed as I passed a fork to her.

"Now, we going to see if you can feed yourself."

Arianna looked at me with determination in her eyes.

I watched as her shaky hands struggled to pick up her food. After a few attempts, she finally got it right. I watched her as she ate and I couldn't help but smile at her.

"I'm going to head to the cafeteria to find something to eat on," I told her as she picked up her cup of sprite with shaky hands.

"Okay, I think I can handle it from here," she replied.

I walked out of her room and was just about to get on the elevator when my phone began to vibrate in my pocket.

I pulled it out and noticed it was Jaleesa calling me.

I answered because I wanted to make sure that she was at least okay. I wasn't the type of nigga who could be cold and intentionally hurt a bitch. I knew the feeling and I didn't want to put anyone through that, not even Jaleesa. She was really a good person and I was concerned for her. I knew a lot about Jaleesa just by being with Arianna. I knew she had been hurt and had started doing niggas just how they had done her in the past. Even though Jaleesa did what she wanted with who she wanted, she always tried to make sure my wife did right by me, and I respected her for that shit.

"Are you okay?" I asked into the phone.

"No, I'm not okay," Jaleesa replied sadly.

The sound of her moving around told me that she was probably in bed.

"Where are you? I need to see you," Jaleesa said.

"I'm at the hospital," I told her.

"I should have known," she replied bitterly.

"Jaleesa, I'm sorry about how things went down."

"Yeah, I bet you are. How is the wifey doing?"

"She is making progress. The doctor believes she will be coming home soon."

Jaleesa became quiet.

"I just feel like the life I'm supposed to be living has been taken from me."

"Jaleesa stop right there."

"You are beautiful, you have so much going for yourself. You going to find that nigga who going to give you the world."

Jaleesa laughed into the phone.

"That man could be with you, but you playing."

I cleared my throat and stepped into the elevator.

"I can't be the one for you Jaleesa, I'm already married."

"Yeah, I know you are, but that don't mean shit these days."

"I'm not leaving my wife Jaleesa, I'm sorry."

"Don't be sorry Dontae, we all must make decisions in our lives, you made yours and now I'm about to make mine."

Something just didn't sit right in my soul after the call with Jaleesa ended. Instead of harping on any of it, I did what I knew was right. I blocked her. I wanted to make things right with my life. Fucking around with Jaleesa wasn't going to lead to anything but drama.

I stepped off the elevator, grabbed me something to eat, and headed back to Arianna's room.

Jaleesa

I felt as if I was losing my mind. The pain that I was feeling inside was something that I had never felt before. I needed someone to talk to that would listen to me. I needed to get a lot of shit off my chest. Holding all this shit in was really fucking with me. I could barely sleep at night because of all the crazy ass dreams that I was having. Just the night before

I had a dream about cutting off Dontae's dick and stabbing him in his throat.

Just thinking back to all the blood that covered my hands really had me feeling queasy to my stomach. The vibe in that dream was if I couldn't have Dontae, Arianna wasn't going to have him either.

So here I was at the Community Health and Behavior Center waiting to be seen by a counselor. I waited for over thirty minutes before I was finally called back into the back.

I took a seat and waited until the therapist was ready to start the session.

She was dressed in a pair of blue jeans, with a white and black Community Health shirt, with a pair of black Nikes. Her long dark brown hair was mixed with a little grey hair and was pulled back in a low ponytail, she looked like she was around the age of fifty, but I wasn't sure. I looked down at her fingers and noticed that she wore no ring.

"Good morning Jaleesa. My name is Ms. Carter and I'm going to be your therapist to help you with all your needs."

I watched her as she flipped through my paperwork and began to start asking me questions about myself. When she was finally done and had all the information, she felt she needed, she finally started asking about the depression that I was suffering.

I gave her the rundown on my relationship with Dontae and his wife Arianna and waited for Ms. Carter to give me her opinion on the matter.

"Jaleesa, I understand you are suffering a heartbreak, this can make anyone depressed, it's very common. With my help, you will be able to push through and get your life back on track."

"No, you don't understand. It's no going back. I feel as if I'm never going to be the same again. It's to the point that I've started having nightmares."

"What kind of nightmares are they?"

"I'm killing his ass or I'm killing her."

Ms. Carter grabbed her notepad and pen and started jotting shit down as I spoke.

"I just can't walk away from him. We made plans to be together and all that shit went to hell and back when Arianna fucked around and got shot in the head and was in a coma for nearly two weeks. He became this devoted husband to a wife who doesn't even love him, when he could have left her ass and been with me. I've always wanted a man like him and have never able to seem to attract them type of niggas. I normally attract fuck boys who want to waste my fucking time and play games."

As I continued to pop off at the mouth, I felt nothing but rage and anger inside. I wanted to tear up some shit. I stood up and paced around her office as I tried to get my emotions in check. Ms. Carter must have felt the energy that I was giving off because she told me to take a few deep breaths and try to calm myself down. I tried to keep my emotions at bay, but it was super hard for me. I needed to fucking express myself and the bitch in front of me had the nerve to look at me like I was crazy.

As I stared at her I began to wonder why in the hell I decided to bring my ass here in the first place. This bitch wasn't helping me express myself. She stayed quiet the whole time and only spoke once and that was to tell me to calm down.

"Jaleesa, you're twenty minutes are now up, but I have written you out two prescriptions. One is to keep you calm and the second one is for antidepressants. Take these pills as instructed and you will be feeling better very soon."

I rolled my eyes.

"Ms. Carter, I didn't bring my ass all the way across town for any medicine. All I wanted to do was talk to someone about the anger and pain that I'm feeling inside. This isn't going to help solve anything."

"Jaleesa, take the medications and give it a chance, you can barely sit through the whole section without walking around and throwing things, this is just our first session and I can sense that you have so many feelings that you need to sort out. The medication will bring them down to the point that they are manageable."

I laughed in her face.

I leaned over her desk and looked into her hazel brown eyes.

"You haven't been in love like I've been in love and you ain't never felt the type of shit that I feel for this nigga. So, don't fucking tell me how I should be feeling."

I snatched the paper off her desk and walked out of her office. I walked angrily to my car and hopped in. I beat my hand up against my steering wheel a few times before I finally maneuvered my car into the heavy traffic. I lit me a cigarette and rolled my window down as (*Rich The Kid*) blasted from my speakers. I didn't want to go home right then, I knew if I went home, I wasn't going to do shit but cry and be depressed so I decided to take a drive. I didn't know where I was going, until I pulled up at the hospital fifteen minutes later. I sat there with my engine running with tears rolling down my face. I needed help, Ms. Carter wasn't lying about that shit. All the places I could have gone in Warner Robins, I had come to the very place where I had gotten my heart broken.

I wiped the tears from my eyes as the bad thoughts began to strongly kick in. I wanted nothing more than to get out my car, go to Arianna's room and choke the bitch out. Maybe if she was out of the way maybe then Dontae would see me and forget about her ass. You can't be with a bitch if they're dead. Just when I was about to get out my car and do the unthinkable my phone started vibrating on the passenger seat.

I grabbed it quickly just to see if Dontae had changed his mind and was deciding to reach out to me, but once I saw Buck number my heart was yet again shattered.

I debated to pick up or not. The last time I had heard from Buck, I had fucked him and told him to get the fuck out of my house. To be honest, I didn't think that he would ever reach back out to me for a long time, after I had dogged him like I had. Now I was beginning to realize that these niggas out here weren't looking for a bitch who was going to love them the right way and treat them like a fucking King. Nall, they wanted a bitch to dog them and not give a fuck about them.

Instead of ignoring his call, I picked up just to see what he wanted.

"Yeah," I said into the phone with an attitude.

"Damn, I'm just calling to see how your ass was doing, but apparently I called you at the wrong time."

I closed my eyes and counted to ten as I tried to calm myself down.

"I'm good, what about you?"

"I'm straight, I just wanted to come through to see you for a minute."
"Are you busy?"

I stared at the hospital for a few moments and debated if I should go inside and take the bitch out or if I should leave the shit alone and go be with Buck.

"Did you hear me?" he asked.

"I heard, and nall I ain't busy."

"Cool, give me thirty minutes, I will be pulling up at your crib. I'm bringing us some weed to smoke and maybe we can watch something on Netflix."

"Alright," I replied before disconnecting the call.

Arianna and Dontae were both lucky that Buck had called me, so we could chill. I needed a good blunt to smoke and Buck had the good shit. I needed to relieve the stress that I was feeling inside so choosing to take my ass home, instead of walking my ass into the hospital and ending her life sounded like the best option.

I made it back to my apartment ten minutes later and headed inside. I grabbed me a wine glass and poured myself some red wine just before taking a seat on my living room couch. I grabbed the remote and was surfing Netflix when Buck knocked on the door. As soon as I let Buck in, I could smell the weed on him.

"Damn, you look like shit, what in the hell happened to you?" Buck asked curiously.

"None of your fucking business," I replied with an attitude.

He shook his head at my comment and flopped down on the couch as he began to roll our blunts.

"I already know what's up with your ass, you look like a nigga done broke your heart. That's a painful feeling shorty," he said as he licked the blunt and lit it.

He took a long puff and passed it to me.

"Can we not talk about this shit."

"I'm just saying shorty, you have a strong ass personality. Can't every nigga deal with your attitude."

"Just because you can't deal with me, don't mean another nigga can't. Do me a favor and shut the fuck up, my attitude isn't the issue that I'm hurting over here."

"Then why are you hurting?"

I took a puff from the blunt and closed my eyes as the smoke filled my lungs.

"You might as well talk to me, I don't want to be seeing your ass on the news for taking a nigga out. Ya'll females are crazy and emotional, ya'll snap quick."

"I went to see a therapist today. I tried to talk to her ass about my feelings and my fears, but the bitch wasn't listening, instead, she wrote me a prescription for some antidepressants."

Buck chuckled.

"You don't need all that shit, all you need is a new man to fuck on, he will take your mind off that lame ass nigga."

I glanced at him for a moment.

"Shid, I ain't talking about myself. I'm talking about any other nigga that you may find attractive. Fuck on someone new, that's your fucking therapy. Good dick fixes everything."

For the first time in a very long time, I laughed.

"See there you go, I finally can see that beautiful smile."

"Thanks for checking up on me."

"You know you my shorty, I'm going to always look out for you. Even though you treat a nigga bad most times, I wouldn't trade you for anybody. I may not be able to please you sexually, but I damn sure can be your friend when you need one."

"You may not set my soul on fire. But sex isn't everything, just having a friend that I can talk to about my feelings is good enough for me."

"Finally, you realize what is most important, our friendship," Buck whispered to me.

Just hearing him telling me that he was always going to look out for me really put me in my feelings. When I began to think back to when I first met Buck three years earlier, I finally realized that no matter what I did or said to him, he had always been there in my corner, holding me down. This time wasn't going to be any different.

Instead of thinking about Dontae and Arianna, I got high as fuck and laid down on Buck's lap and talked to him about all my problems until him and I both fell into a deep sleep.

Arianna

Two Weeks Later...

The doctor had been correct. It took no longer than two weeks for me to regain my strength. Even though I wasn't one hundred percent just yet, I was still at ninety-five percent which was good enough that the doctor felt it was okay to finally discharge me. As the sun penetrated my face, I felt nothing but joy inside my heart. I was finally free and able to go back to my home. Dontae held me by the hand as he opened the car door for me and tried to help me slide inside.

"Dontae, you ain't got to do all this no more, I can do for myself now," I joked him.

Dontae smirked at me just before I slid into the car.

"I don't mind by doing for my beautiful wife."

Just being next to him and being in his presence, filled my life with love and commitment. I came into the hospital broken and came out ready to love the man who had committed himself to me.

"Where are we going?" I asked Dontae as he pulled into traffic.

"I can't tell you that, you will see when we get there."

I stared out the window and closed my eyes for a quick moment as the hot wind blew across my face.

Twenty minutes later, Dontae shook me and told me that we had made it to our destination.

I slid out of the car and stood there for the longest moment as I admired the sparkling water and the imitation sand. It was as if I was in a trance with the beauty and the peace of the lake.

"While you were sleeping, I stopped to get us some lunch, we are having sandwiches, wine, and a fruit tray you will die for."

Dontae grabbed me by one hand as he clutched the bag of food with his other.

After we had found us the perfect spot, Dontae placed a blanket on the ground and we took a seat across from one another. The birds chirped in the distance and there wasn't a soul in sight to ruin this romantic moment.

Dontae fixed me a plate and poured me a small glass of Pink Moscato as we talked and laughed with one another. I took the first bite of my turkey breast sandwich and closed my eyes as I savored the taste.

"Finally, I get food that doesn't take like death. God, I've missed this."

Dontae laughed as he watched me devour my whole meal. I sipped on my wine as I ate my grapes and strawberries.

"Your so fucking beautiful," Dontae complimented me as he admired me from afar.

I couldn't help but blush at his compliments.

"Thank you, baby."

"I'm just so glad you finally home and we're together."

"I wouldn't have it any other way," I said truthfully.

I held my breath as he leaned in to kiss me. My heart felt it was about to beat out of my chest and my juice box was aching to be touched. It had been so long since I had fucked and my body was letting me know it was time to give my pussy a workout.

As the kiss deepened, I pulled him closer to me. He caressed my body with his hands as our tongues explored each other mouths. The kiss broke a few moments later, but that was only to push the food that we had been eating out of our way. Next thing you know, I'm laid down on my back with him between my legs. I closed my eyes as he kissed and sucked on my neck. I was so sexually aroused that I didn't even give a fuck if someone saw us. I wanted some dick and I wanted it right at that moment.

My pussy was soaking wet by the time he pulled down my booty shorts and slid off my yellow thong. He slid his hands under my yellow tank top and pinched each of my nipples just before he started sucking on them.

"Fuck," I heard myself moan.

My heart pounded, and my stomach felt as if I had butterflies in them. When he slid between my thighs and began sucking on my pussy, I already knew it wasn't going to take me long to reach my peak. I closed my eyes tightly as I fucked his face.

"Shit baby, right there," I heard myself moan out to him.

When he slid a finger into my honey pot, I heard myself cry out as he finger fucked me until I creamed all over him. My pussy was throbbing and it seemed as if Dontae couldn't unzip his pants fast enough.

This was the first time since I've known Dontae that I ever felt this sexual chemistry that I was feeling. I never had the urge of wanting him to fuck me so badly until now. It seemed like before the accident we weren't in sync with each other bodies. He couldn't please me and I guess it goes back to the part where I just didn't have any love for him. Now that my feelings had changed, I was ready to see just how good his dick game was. When he slid his wood deep into me, I held on to him as he deep stroked me. Even though Dontae dick wasn't big like I preferred, he made up for it when he started pounding inside me.

My eyes were literally rolling to the back of my head as he fucked me. I was near tears when he pushed my legs to the back of my head and started beating my pussy down. He played with my titties as he stared deep into my eyes.

I felt the love and I instantly climaxed off just that.

"Yeah baby, give me all that creamy shit," he told me as he slowed his strokes.

After I had creamed all over his dick, he pulled out of me and flipped me over. I positioned myself on my knees and arched my back. I played with my clit as he slid into me from the back. I cried out his name as he blew my back out. This nigga wasn't playing with me, he was giving me all that he had. My pussy juices were leaking down my thighs as Dontae worked his magic on my kitty. I screamed out when he yanked me by my hair and continued to drill into me.

A few strokes later he pulled his dick out my love tunnel and spilled his seed on my back.

"Fuck," we both said in union.

Dontae grabbed the paper towels that he had brought with him and hurried to wipe me clean. We put back on our clothes and laid there a little while longer. We were both tired and my body felt weak as fuck but it was all in a good way. We stood up about twenty minutes later, so we could head home. My feet were shaky at first but I quickly regained my balance when Dontae gave me his hand to hold.

We threw our trash into the lake's garbage cans and headed back to where we were parked. On the way home, I couldn't help but stare out the window and see my life unfolding right before my eyes.

Since the accident so much had changed for me, my feelings had changed, my outlook on life had changed, and I felt like a better person. I always stressed about wanting to be in love and happy and here I was sitting beside the man who I never would have thought I could love. My life was good, it was finally perfect.

Jaleesa

Depression was real, and it was something I found myself struggling with. I went from dogging niggas to being so deeply infatuated with Dontae that I could barely see straight. The fact that he had pushed me away fucked with my ego. I mean damn, I was a fine ass bitch, I had education, I knew how to hold down a job, and I could suck a nigga skin off his dick. I had nothing but love and loyalty to give to his ass and for him to just turn all of it down really fucked me up inside. I lit a cigarette and tried to calm my nerves, but I couldn't take my mind off the heartbreak that I was feeling inside.

I grabbed my cell phone and logged into my Facebook account only to want to throw my phone across the room. Just seeing Dontae and Arianna hugged up in a picture brought tears to my eyes. The sound of my phone smashing against the wall didn't even phase me. I was just that zoned out and wasn't really thinking right. I didn't want to think logical, I wanted to stay in the fairytale dream of finding a nigga who was going to love me and give me anything that my heart desired.

Arianna was back home and she was finally getting herself back together, I knew deep down that I had lost the battle of making Dontae mine. I had just learned the hard way that when nigga loved a bitch it didn't matter how bad they dogged them or did them if they truly loved them, they weren't going to leave them for no one, not even if they knew they could have something better.

I had the urge to call someone anyone to come over and beat my pussy down but the thought of someone touching me quickly made me feel that fucking someone else wasn't going to take my mind off Dontae or Arianna. I slid off my bed, headed towards the kitchen, and poured me a glass of wine. I went into the bathroom to run me some bath water, hoping that this will ease my mind. I sat by the tub poured me some scented bubbles into the water and watched as the hot water filled up the tub. After the tub was ready, I took off my bed clothes and slid inside.

I closed my eyes and tried to relax but I couldn't stop seeing Dontae. Tears began to roll down my cheeks and they wouldn't stop. I grabbed the wine glass that was filled with red wine and drunk the entire glass. I needed something to take the pain away. I soaked in the tub for nearly a hour before I stepped out to dry myself off. I stared at myself in the mirror for the longest time. My eyes were red and puffy from crying myself to sleep the night before. I brushed my hair back, brushed my teeth, and found something comfortable to wear around the house.

My stomach growled and I knew it was time for me to eat something. I had been so into my feelings that I couldn't even remember the last time I had really eaten something. Just the thought of food had me feeling sick as hell. I headed into the kitchen to see if could find something to much on, but when I looked into the fridge, I noticed that I needed to buy some grocery.

I groaned and slammed the fridge door shut.

I was dressed in a pair of white shorts, with a pink shirt, I grabbed my pink Nike shoes, and put them on my feet. I grabbed my keys and purse and headed out the door. I needed food, but I wasn't in the mood to cook shit. I maneuvered my way into traffic and was on my way to get something from McDonald's when my phone began to ring.

When I noticed it was my therapist calling, I ignored the call. Five minutes later the bitch was calling back.

"Jaleesa, this is Ms. Carter from the Community Health and Behavior Center."

"I know who this is, what do you want?"

"I'm just calling to make sure that you are okay. Have you been taking the medicine that I prescribed to you two weeks ago?"

I became quiet.

"Jaleesa, you must take the medicine that I prescribed."

"Look, lady, I don't need that shit. I just needed someone to talk to because I was going through a lot of shit in my fucking life."

"Jaleesa are you okay? You sound upset. Do you need to come in so we can talk?"

"No, I don't need to come in. Matter fact I don't need your services."

"Jaleesa, please don't do this, you need help, you are really suffering emotionally, I don't want you to hurt anyone or yourself."

"I'm not going to hurt anyone. Bye, I got to go."

"Jaleesa..."

I didn't even give her ass time to say nothing else before I hung up. I hated that I had even contacted the bitch now. All she did was judge me and imply that I was looney. The last thing I needed was to be on some medicine to tell me how I should feel. These were my own fucking feelings and I was going to deal with them the best way that I knew how.

I waited in the McDonald's drive thru nearly ten minutes before I could grab my food. After making it back home I took a seat in the living room but the urge to eat had left my body. Instead, I stared at a movie that was playing on Netflix. I was watching it, but I wasn't comprehending shit that was being said.

I pushed the half-eaten food from McDonald's away from me before I grabbed my phone to see if I could at least try to contact Dontae. My heart stopped and went still when I found out that he had blocked me.

I completely lost it. He really was done with me to the point that he made sure that I couldn't contact him. The shit hurt me to my soul. Instead of leaving the shit alone, I called his ass by blocking my number. He picked up on the first ring. I heard Arianna in the background laughing which irked my soul.

"Who this?" Dontae asked.

"This Jaleesa," I replied softly.

"Jaleesa, why are you calling me? I blocked you for a reason. Arianna is home. We trying to build something, I can't be distracted."

"You broke my heart," I cried into the phone.

"Jaleesa, I honestly didn't know that you felt this serious about me. I can't give you what you want. I'm sorry if I hurt you."

"No, you're not sorry, but you soon will be."

I ended the call and knew exactly what I had to do.

I was crying my eyes out and could barely see straight. My heart was broken and there wasn't anything that I could to make me feel better. No one understood the pain one feels when they wanted to be with someone who didn't want the same thing. I felt as if my life was over. I wanted to end the pain, I wanted to die. I had nothing or no one to live for. I had no family, I had lost my best friend because of this shit, and the one man I thought would hold me down had turned on me as well. The pain and heartbreak that I was feeling were about to finally be over.

I didn't bother by wiping the tears from my eyes, instead I headed into the kitchen to grab a kitchen knife. I went back into the living room and sat back on my couch with the knife in my hand. Snot ran down my nose and the tears covered my face. I was looking a hot mess, but I felt dead inside. I felt defeated and I was ready to end it all. I didn't think twice about slitting both of my wrists. As the blood began to pour out of my body, I closed my eyes and I said a silent prayer to the man above.

"I may didn't find love in this lifetime, but I pray the next lifetime I do, God please forgive me for what I'm about to do."

I sat there bleeding out as my entire life flashed before my eyes. So much I wish I could go back and redo, but it just wasn't possible. As the tears began to stain my cheeks, I closed my eyes and finally felt at peace.

Epilogue

Arianna

Learning that Jaleesa had taken her own life really hurt me to my soul. I never wanted any of this to happen and yet it did. To lose my best friend was heartbreaking. The pain and the hurt that I was feeling was always going to stick with me. Even though Jaleesa and I had fallen out due to the Dontae situation I never would wish death on her. Yes, she had lost her way. She wanted to have this fairytale love and that didn't happen for her, I just wished things would have turned out differently.

I wiped the tears from my eyes as I the pastor asked for all of us to say our final goodbyes. Dontae and I slowly walked towards her cherry wood coffin as the rain poured down from the sky.

"I'm sorry Jaleesa for everything, may you rest in peace," I whispered.

"I'm so sorry Jaleesa, please forgive me," Dontae whispered sadly as tears fell from his eyes.

My mother stood in the distance and watched us. I walked over to her and noticed she had been crying.

"I'm going to miss her," my mother replied emotionally.

"We all are," I replied.

There was no way I could tell my mother the true reason of what all that Jaleesa and I had been going through before she took her own life. I didn't want to feel that Dontae and I were the reason why she ended it all, but deep down inside I knew Dontae and I had a lot to do with it.

Just when the pastor was about to say the prayer to put her at rest, I spotted Buck walking towards her coffin. I knew he was probably taking her death hard. Even though Buck and Jaleesa had this love-hate relationship, he stuck by her through the good times and the bad times. He overlooked her shortcomings and continued to stick by her until she took her last breath.

Even though it was pouring down rain and the wind was blowing, I could still hear Buck crying out Jaleesa's name.

"Jaleesa, why did you have to leave me? I miss you so fucking much!" Buck kept yelling out.

Everyone was very emotional, but Buck really took it the hardest. The pastor eventually had to get one of his men to grab Buck and pull him away from Jaleesa's casket so he could get calmed down.

Lightning flashed across the sky and the tornado siren went off. Everyone started to panic.

"Have everyone said their goodbyes?" the pastor asked.

Everyone responded that they had and the pastor said a small prayer for Jaleesa before everyone was free to leave.

"The weather is about to get bad and I want each one of you to make it home safely!" the pastor shouted to all of us.

Dontae, my mother, and I ran towards our car and hopped inside. My mother slid into the back while Dontae took the wheel. As we drove home, I noticed that my mother was very quiet.

"Mom are you okay?" I asked her with concern.

"I'm just sitting back here thinking. We never know when it's our time to go or how we going to leave here. I just want to enjoy the little time that I have left on this Earth. I'm just so grateful for so much in life. I'm grateful to have such an amazing daughter and a wonderful son in law. I just want us to live a happy life as a family."

"I love you mom," I told her sweetly.

"I love you more baby."

As I watched the raindrops on the window Dontae took me by my hand and placed tender kisses on fingers.

I gave him a weak smile. He must have seen the sadness in my eyes because he cleared his throat and told me some shit that I'm going to always remember.

"We can't change the past, we can only keep moving and living our lives. I want to spend the rest of my life loving only you."

"The love I have for you gets stronger every day. I'm so glad that I didn't lose you." I admitted to him.

"You will never have to worry about me going anywhere. I'm always going to be here for you baby." Dontae replied gently.

Even though my heart was in pain about Jaleesa's death it was still filled with the love that Dontae had awaken inside of me.

I became lost in my thoughts as I watched the raindrops run down my window. Love could be powerful and beautiful all at the same time and some people were willing to anything for it, they were even willing to die for it.

Connect With Me On Social Media

Subscribe to my mailing list by visiting my website:
https://www.shaniceb.com/

- Like my Facebook author page:
https://www.facebook.com/ShaniceBTheAuthor/?ref=aymt_homepage_panel

- Join my reader's group on Facebook. I post short stories and sneak peeks of my upcoming novels that I'm working on
https://www.facebook.com/groups/1551748061561216/

- Send me a friend request on Facebook:
https://www.facebook.com/profile.php?Id=100011411930304&__nodl

- Follow me on Instagram:
https://www.instagram.com/shaniceb24/?hl=en

<u>About The Author</u>

Shanice B was born and raised in Georgia. At the age of nine years old, she discovered her love for reading and writing. At the age of ten, she wrote her first short story and read it in front of her classmates, who fell in love with her wild imagination. After graduating high school, Shanice decided to pursue her career in Early Childhood Education. After giving birth to her son, Shanice decided it was time to pick up her pen and get back to what she loved the most.

She is the author of over twenty books and is widely known for her bestselling four-part series titled Who's Between the Sheets: Married to A Cheater. Shanice is also the author of the three-part series, Love Me If You Can, and three standalone novels titled Stacking It Deep: Married to My Paper, A Love So Deep: Nobody Else Above you, and Love, I Thought You Had My Back. In November of 2016, Shanice decided to try her hand at writing a two-part street lit series titled Loving My Mr. Wrong: A Street Love Affair. Shanice resides in Georgia with her family and her six-year-old son.

Now Available on Amazon!!!

Karly McAdams believes she is living the perfect life with her longtime boyfriend Javier, but things take a swift turn when tragedy hits. With a broken heart and with the desperation to move on with her life, Karly decides to fly to Minnesota to spend Christmas with her family. After arriving back to her hometown, her mother introduces her to a model named Lindsey Mitchell. Lindsey has been happily married to her husband Carter for five years. She loves her man from the bottom of her heart and believes he feels the same about her until she learns of his betrayal. With her heart shattered to pieces, she feels she has no one to lean on until

Karly makes it clear that she can confide in her.

As Lindsey and Karly's friendship becomes stronger, a full-blown romance occurs that neither can ignore. As their love for each other deepens, Lindsey will eventually have to make a choice between her family and the love she has for Karly.

Will their love survive, or will it wither and die?

Now Available On Amazon!!!!

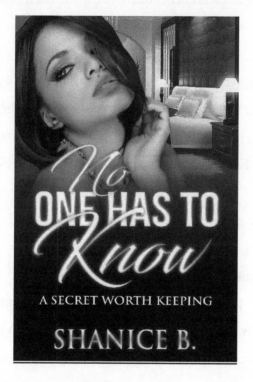

"Sometimes when you think you know a person, that's when you learn that you never knew them at all."

Layla and her brother Lamar have always been close, but their relationship soon starts to become rocky when Layla leaves her abusive boyfriend and moves in with Lamar and his girlfriend, Promise. Lamar believes he's doing the right thing by stepping in and helping his baby sister, but he soon will see that he has made a fatal mistake.

When Promise learns that her boyfriend Lamar has cheated on her, Promise feels as if her perfect world has been shattered right before her eyes. As she tries to mend her broken heart, she soon realizes that this will not be an easy task because she can't let go of the pain of her man hurting her.

Promise and Layla are both having a hard time coping with their love lives. They both feel as if they don't have anyone in their corner to help them get through their difficult time. When they realize that they're all each other have, an unlikely friendship begins to bloom that is unbreakable.

After a sultry night involving too many drinks, their close friendship turns into a hot steamy love affair.

They both know if Lamar ever finds out about their secret, all hell will break loose, but they will soon conclude that what Lamar don't know can't hurt him. Will Promise and Layla be able to keep their love a secret or will Lamar recognize the red flags that symbolize something just isn't right?

Now Available On Amazon!!!!

Meet Me In My Bedroom Volume 2 is a collection of erotic love stories that will pull you in from the very first page. These erotic stories are all hot steamy reads that are centered around romantic relationships. Volume 2 will make your panties wet and have you begging for more. Read at your own risk. Enjoy!!!

Now Available On Amazon!!!

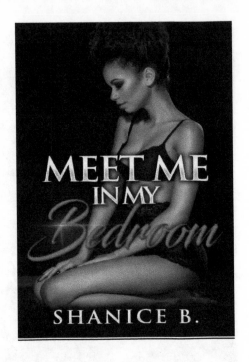

Meet Me In My Bedroom will have you glued to your Kindle from the very first page.

These erotic love stories are steamy hot reads that are centered around romantic relationships.

Each love story is jaw dropping and will have you begging for more.

Read at your own risk. Enjoy!!

Now Available On Amazon!!!

QUICK NOTE: This is a twelve-thousand-word erotic short story. If you are looking for something sexy and quick to read, then this will be the perfect read for you.

Heartbroken over her ex leaving her for another woman, Kira seems to not be able to shake her bruised ego. When Kira's best friend Shonda persuades her to have a girl's night out to take her mind off her heartbreak, Kira's life will forever be changed.

In walks Jacolby...

When Kira and Jacolby lock eyes on each other their burning desire and lust for one another is what they feel. Kira is FEENIN' for some dope dick and Jacolby just happens to be the man who is eager to please her inside and outside of the bedroom.

Once Jacolby dicks her down, Kira finds herself falling for him hard and fast and there is nothing she can do about it but let it happen.

When Kira's ex magically reappears, she must make a decision. Will she go back to the man that has broken her heart or will she remain with the one man who has swept her off her feet and made her feel things she has never felt before?

JUN 3 - 2019

CPSIA information can be obtained
at www.ICGtesting.com
Printed in the USA
LVHW041605010419
612558LV00003B/543/P

9 781796 433555